A Bronx Tale 3

**Lock Down Publications and Ca$h
Presents**
A Bronx Tale 3
A Novel by *Ghost*

Lock Down Publications
P.O. Box 870494
Mesquite, Tx 75187

Visit our website @
www.lockdownpublications.com

Copyright 2019 A Bronx Tale 3

First Edition May 2019
Printed in the United States of America

This is a work of fiction. Names, characters, places, and incidents either are products of the author's imagination or are used fictitiously. Any similarity to actual events or locales or persons, living or dead, is entirely coincidental.

Lock Down Publications
Like our page on Facebook: Lock Down Publications @
www.facebook.com/lockdownpublications.ldp
Cover design and layout by: **Dynasty Cover Me**
Book interior design by: **Shawn Walker**
Edited by: **Lauren Burton**

Stay Connected with Us!

Text **LOCKDOWN** to 22828 to stay up-to-date with new releases, sneak peaks, contests and more…

Thank you.

Submission Guideline.

Submit the first three chapters of your completed manuscript to ldpsubmissions@gmail.com, subject line: Your book's title. The manuscript must be in a .doc file and sent as an attachment. Document should be in Times New Roman, double spaced and in size 12 font. Also, provide your synopsis and full contact information. If sending multiple submissions, they must each be in a separate email.

Have a story but no way to send it electronically? You can still submit to LDP/Ca$h Presents. Send in the first three chapters, written or typed, of your completed manuscript to:

LDP: Submissions Dept
Po Box 870494
Mesquite, Tx 75187

DO NOT send original manuscript. Must be a duplicate.

Provide your synopsis and a cover letter containing your full contact information.

Only if your submission is **approved**, will you then get a response letter.

Thanks for considering LDP and Ca$h Presents.

Ghost

Chapter 1

Ari hit me up ten days after she left Misty's crib. It was five o'clock in the morning and storming like crazy outside. Misty had been the one to hand me the phone. She stood on the side of the bed wit' her hand on her hip as if she didn't want me talking to her. I frowned, then ignored her ass.

"Yo, what's good, Ari? Where you been at?" I rubbed the cold out of my eyes and yawned. I was feeling extremely tired this morning, and all my injuries were killing me. I needed a few of those Percocet in my life. I would hit Misty's ass up for a few after I hung the phone up.

"It's time, Jahmani. I got everything set up the way it needs to be. Dough Boy and P.T. is holding Lonnie in a duplex over in Harlem. I'm texting you the address right now. I want you to meet me there. I'll let you in through the back door when the coast is clear. You need to get in, handle your business, and get back out, though. They're going to be expecting a delivery from Beans. He's supposed to show up with a bunch of his goons sometime today, but I don't know when."

Misty grabbed the phone and clicked it onto speaker. She frowned at me and mugged my iPhone 8. She shook her head and mouthed the words *I don't trust this bitch.*

"Yo, ma, why are they moving her out of the Bronx? Whose idea is this? And have you seen her?" I asked, rising out of the bed and sliding my legs into my jeans. I needed to feel Ari just a little bit more. There was no telling how she was feeling after finding out I had been the one who killed her brother and I was fucking Misty. They said hell hath no fury like a woman scorned. I wondered if Ari was scorned. I wondered if she had some vindictive shit up her sleeve. I wondered what her angle was.

"Yeah, I've seen her. I gave her breakfast this morning and

a bath last night, per P.T.'s wishes. She's still beautiful. Lost a few pounds from the last time I'd seen her, but appears healthy, nonetheless. And I think it was Beans' idea to move her out to Harlem. They are up to something in the Bronx, and he's feeling like the spot they were once in will become a target by both enemies and the police."

"Yeah, a'ight. What time are you talking, shorty?" Something didn't feel right. I felt like there was more at play than what she was letting on. I paced back and forth in front of the phone that sat on the dresser, trying to collect my thoughts.

"Four. Four should be good because we're supposed to leave here around two-thirty. I'll do my part when it comes to his mind. Keep him discombobulated. Dough Boy is another story, though. That fool is a head case, and him and I don't get along. I think he's on the down-low because he appears to hate all women. Before you get at P.T., you're going to have to take care of him. Trust me on this." She paused. "We're on the first floor, so when I let you in through the back door, you'll go right in through the kitchen, and they'll be set up right there at the table in the dining room, whipping Beans' heroin."

"Bitch, what's in it for you? You ain't finna do all this shit for nothing. What the fuck is your thirsty-ass getting out of all of this?" Misty snapped before I rushed to her and placed my hand over her mouth.

Ari was quiet, and then I could hear her exhale loudly into the phone. "Really, Jahmani? You got her listening to our calls now? That's how you're getting down on me?"

I grabbed Misty by the back of the neck and threw her out of the room and into the hallway. "Bitch, stay yo' ass out here until I'm done since you can't keep your mouth closed," I snapped, ready to spank her ass until she screamed for me to stop. I was that heated by her outburst.

"But, daddy, I was just –" she began.

I slammed the door in her face and had to calm myself down.

"Jahmani! Jahmani! Did you hear what I said?" Ari hollered into the phone. "Hell-o?"

I picked it up. "Nall, I ain't hear what you said. What's good?"

"In exchange for me doing this stuff for you, I want her ass."

"What do you mean by that?" I inquired, needing to make sure.

"What I mean is I wanna beat her to death. She's too far into our business, probably jumping your bones every chance she gets, and on top of that, my back ain't been the same ever since she hit me with that baseball bat. That's the deal: you get Lonnie, and I get to do whatever I want to do to Misty. Deal or no deal?"

***

Four hours later, Misty pulled her Jeep Grand Cherokee up a block away from where we were set to meet with Ari. She threw the Jeep in park and looked over to me. "I can't believe we're about to trust this bitch, Jahmani. Do you realize this could be a set-up in which we both lose our lives? I mean, she hates me, and you killed her brother. Why would she go all out of her way to help you get your niece back? This just doesn't make sense. Can't you see that?" She placed her hand on my thigh.

I cocked both of my Glocks and put them back on my waist. I had nothing but murder flowing through my mind. I kept seeing the image of my mother's slain body in my head, then the smirk on P.T.'s face when I went to the door, trying to get Ari back. I wanted to blow his head off just on the strength of him fucking my woman. I was on some sucker shit, and I couldn't even deny it. "Look, Misty, what you're saying makes sense, but at the same time, I gotta handle my business. These muthafuckas killed my mother and had my niece for almost two months. It's only a matter of time before they kill her, too. I mean, I still don't know why they've kept her alive this long."

"That's what I'm saying, you don't even know if she is alive. For all you know, she could be already dead, and you could be walking into a trap. I could lose you, and all for what? I say we get the fuck outta here, leave New York tonight, and just drive until we're far away from here. I got some people in North Carolina, people Ari don't know about. We can go there, and you can start over, baby. Please, listen to me. Ari is going to be the death of you." She grabbed my wrist and kissed the back of my hand, rubbing her face into the palm of it. "Please."

I sat there for a moment, thinking everything over that she'd said. Would it be smart to turn the Jeep around and drive away from avenging my mother's murder? Should I leave my niece to fend for herself, essentially leaving her to die? What about Linx? Should I forgo that beef, let him walk away scot-free? Could I turn my back on my past and start somewhere fresh? Was it smart to leave the city of New York behind and enter North Carolina blindly beside Misty? How much did I really care about her? And was the life of Lonnie a fair exchange for Misty's? Could I stand to trust Ari to hold up her side of things?

"Baby, please say something to me. You've been quiet for ten minutes," Misty said, placing her hand on the side of my face.

My phone vibrated with a text from Ari. *It's time.* Those were the only words that came across my screen.

I took a deep breath and slid my phone back into my

pocket. "I gotta handle my bidness and let the cards fall where they may, so let's go," I ordered, feeling my heart pounding in my chest.

Misty blinked and tears rolled down her cheeks. "I got a feeling we're making a mistake. But, like I said, you lead, and I'll follow. So, let's do this."

She put the Jeep in drive and pulled it into the alley that led to the duplex I was set to meet Ari in.

*

Ghost

Chapter 2

Misty wiped the tears from her eyes and took a deep breath. She glanced down the alley, shielded her eyes from her sunlight, shook her head, and sighed. "Jahmani, I don't care what you are about to tell me, you're not going in there alone. I don't trust this bitch, and if she's setting you up, then I'm going in there with you and we're going to meet our deaths together. It's as simple as that." She grabbed her purse from the back seat and pulled out a .380 handgun, lifted her blouse, and tucked the pistol into her waistband like she'd seen me do so many times before with bigger, more powerful weapons. She reached for the handle of the door and made an attempt to get out.

I stopped her. "Shawty, you need to chill right here and keep this engine running in case it is some kind of a setup. Ain't no sense in both of us walking into a trap. I'm finna go in here and see what the move is. If shawty on some bullshit, or if you hear a bunch of shots fired and don't see me emerge in less than two minutes, you pull off and go on wit' yo' life. You know how this New York shit is, shawty. Here today, gone tomorrow." I mugged the duplex from a distance and prepared myself for the deadly fate I might be walking into.

Misty jumped out of her seat and over to mine. She fell on her knees and buried her face into my lap. "Daddy. Please. Please, listen to me. Don't trust this bitch. I don't want to lose you. You've just become a part of my life. I can't be without you already, so don't make me," she cried.

I swallowed the lump in my throat, pulled her up, and held her face in my hands. "Shawty, chill the fuck out. A'ight? Now, you gotta woman-up. This is where we are right now. I'm in a fucked-up position, but most importantly, so is my li'l niece. I gotta rescue her. I gotta get her out of that sticky

13

situation. She's innocent and ain't never really had a chance in this world. I gotta get her backs and try to make things right. It'll be the one good thing I've done in life. She deserves that." I looked into Misty's pretty eyes. "Baby, I need you to be strong. Daddy got this. You hear me? I got this shit, boo." I kissed her lips even though she had a trace of snot forming at the top of her lip.

Her lips pressed to mine and she moaned. Her eyes closed. She shook her head in disagreement. "Baby, I don't want you to do this, but I can't stop you, either. I see that. I'll do whatever you want me to do, long as you know I got your back." She kissed me again.

I held her for a moment. She felt good in my arms. Her scent was all feminine and still forbidden to me because she was Ari's cousin. I couldn't wait to finish handling my bidness so I could get back between them thick-ass thighs of hers. "I appreciate you, baby. Now, what I want you to do when I get out of this Jeep is to pull into the alley and park in the garage right over there. But park so the front of the Jeep is facing outward. Keep the engine running, and like I said, when you hear the first round of gunfire, you give me three minutes. If I'm not back out to you in three minutes, then you pull away, and you g'on to North Carolina by yourself and act like you've never met me."

This got her extremely emotional. "No! Fuck that, baby. I'm not going to do that. I'm not going to act like I've never met you, Jahmani. You're a good man. Look at what you're doing! You're putting your life on the line for a little girl that's not even yours. She's just your niece. You've been through so much, Daddy. I know if I can get you away from all of this, you're going to be one hell of a man to me. I just know you will be." She was crying again.

I didn't know what to say or feel. I needed to be in a

murderous zone, cold-hearted and unfeeling, but Misty was carrying me in an emotional rollercoaster. She had me ready to snatch her li'l ass up and spoon instead of grabbing my two Glocks to smoke some shit. I had to snap out of it, had to put Lonnie at the forefront of my brain. If it was God's will, I would get the chance to really rock wit' Misty after I came from under this situation. But as it stood, I needed to finish the task at hand.

I kissed her lips again. "Baby, I got this. Do like the fuck I said. I'm bred by these streets. I know how to conduct myself accordingly, and if you gon' be my bitch, then you gon' do the same. Get yo' ass over into that driver seat and be ready." I kissed her again, my heart heavy for her. I felt something already, and I didn't even wanna admit that shit. Damn, she was fucking with my mind.

Misty nodded her head and eased over into the driver's seat. Her eyelids were red from crying, cheeks streaked with tears. She wiped her face with her right hand. "Okay, daddy. Just please be careful. I need you. You have no idea how much."

I grabbed her thigh and squeezed it, opened the door to the passenger's side, and jumped out into the alley. I was already beginning to sweat under the bullet-proof vest, but the rays from the sun only made things that much worse. I ain't gon' even lie and say I wasn't afraid of what I was getting ready to walk into, because I was. I wasn't fearful of death – never had been. Everybody had to die. I just feared how I was set to go out. I didn't wanna suffer or no shit like that. If I was to go, I was hoping it was quick and not so painful, but that chapter had already been written by the Lord above, so it was what it was.

I sent Ari a quick text letting her know I was two minutes away and to meet me at the back door, then I jogged down the alley and tried my best to stay obscured. Luckily there was nobody in the filthy alley. It had garbage and dirty clothes all over it. There was also more than one assumedly stolen car inside the alley. The cars had been stripped bare. The atmosphere smelled like baked garbage, and there was a dead cat right in the center of the alley.

Right before I got to the backyard of the duplex, I removed one of my Glocks and eased into the yard. The grass was crunchy. I looked right and left to see if anything looked out of the ordinary. As far as I could tell, everything looked normal.

Instead of going right to the back door, I jogged to the side of the house and listened. I needed to see if I could hear anything coming from inside, but it was quiet. Somewhere toward the front of the house, probably on the street somewhere, I could hear somebody playing their car's system.

I jogged to the back of the house and waited, closed my eyes briefly, and took a deep breath. My heart was beating harder than a locked out lover in the middle of the night. I waited for five full minutes, then came the sound of the locks turning on the door. I took two steps back and raised my gun, ready to blow a muthafucka's head off. If this was a setup, I had plans to take more than a few out before I met my demise.

When the final bolt unlocked on the door, it was pulled open. Ari stuck her pretty face out. Her curls hung by her cheeks. Her perfume floated over to me, incarcerated my senses, and held me captive. The scent of her had always been a problem for me.

She looked first to her left, then spotted me when she checked the right side. She jumped back into the doorway and held her chest. She stepped out of the hallway and closed the door as lightly as she could behind her. Her almond-shaped eyes looked into mine. "Jahmani, they been doing dope all morning. Them niggas in there baked. They got about three bricks of Bean's work left to foil up, so they gon' be a minute. However, Lonnie is inside. She's chained to the radiator in the middle bedroom. That fool P.T. just got done tryin' to force her to eat a bologna sandwich. He been handling her real rough. She didn't eat it, either. She's lost a lot of weight. You have to get to her."

I made a move to fly past her. Now that I knew Lonnie was inside, that was all I needed to hear. I was 'bout to go, get my niece, and be on my way.

Ari grabbed my arm. "Hold the phone, nigga. Where is my cousin?" she mugged me.

I pulled my arm away from her. "Shawty, a deal is a deal. If my niece in here and I get her back, you gon' be able to do whatever you wanna do wit' Misty. That shit ain't my concern. Now, let's go before these niggas get wise to what's about to jump off. Come on."

She pulled me again. "Nall, screw that, Jahmani. You said we'd exchange one for one. I get Misty, and you get Lonnie. That's what I agreed to. But it feels like you're going to try and fuck me out of our deal. I should've known you'd get down like this after all the bullshit you've taken me through. Ugh, and I know it's all because of her."

I grabbed her by her collar and slammed her against the back of the house. She beat at my hand. "Ari, we ain't got time for this bullshit right now. I gotta get in there and handle my bidness. I'm gon' hold up my side of the deal. Now, where the fuck are they?"

She slapped at my hand until I released her, straightened her clothes, and frowned at me. "Keep your fuckin' hands to yourself, Jahmani. I am not your child." She curled her upper lip. "They're sitting in the living room. As soon as you step out of the kitchen, you'll see them. There is work all over the table, and they're bagging and foiling Bean's stuff. You have to act quick. Come on." She bumped me out of the way.

Something about all of this just didn't feel right. I brought out both Glocks and said a silent prayer, asking Him to help me get through this mission and come out on the other end with myself and my niece alive and well. I didn't know if prayers from a killer made it to Heaven, but I was about to find out. I was also looking forward to being covered in sin 'cause I didn't give a fuck what went down. I was about to body these niggas with no remorse.

Ari stepped into the house and peeked up the stairs. She waved me over. I stepped inside the house and brushed past her. It smelled like cigarette smoke and her perfume. She closed the door lightly and crept up the stairs. When she got to the inner back door, she placed a finger to her lips and eased it open.

The door creaked. It felt like it was screaming out to the enemies on the other side, warning them they were about to be ambushed by a straight goon.

Ari took ahold of the doorknob and pushed it open a tad bit more. As soon as it was open wide enough for me to slip through, I eased inside, both Glocks ready. There was a cloud of cigarette smoke now. That shit smelled horrible to me. I put a li'l pep in my step and jogged through the kitchen.

When I got to the living room, it was just like she said. There was P.T. and Doughboy sitting at the table, foiling and packaging Bean's work. I sprinted to the table and smacked P.T. in the back of the head with the gun. He slumped to the floor and hollered out in pain. I aimed the other Glock at Doughboy.

"Nigga, where the fuck my li'l niece at? And which one of you bitch-niggas killed my mother?"

Doughboy threw his hands in the air and shot daggers at

Ari. "You punk-ass bitch! You set us up. Wait 'til Beans find out about his shit."

P.T. scooted backward on his ass. Blood ran down his neck. "You bogus, Ari. Bitch, you let this nigga off your brother and still show him loyalty. Fuck type of shit is that?" Ari covered her mouth and stepped into the kitchen. She looked stunned.

"Nigga, I'ma ask y'all this last time, where is my niece?" Now I had one gun aimed at each man.

Doughboy spoke up first. "She in that room right there, cuz. I ain't fucked wit' her. You can take her and bounce. That nigga been whooping her ass all day. I ain't touched her once."

"Aw, that's how you living?" P.T. said, sitting with his back against the wall. "Ask that fuck-nigga who killed your mother, Jahmani, since he so easily offering information. Tell him who slumped his mother, kid?"

Doughboy swallowed. "You and Beans. I ain't have shit to do wit' that, either." Doughboy shifted uncomfortably.

"Son, you lying. You gon' tell that boldface lie like that? Yo, you foul as hell, kid. I should," P.T. made an attempt to get up from the floor.

I saw his movement and brought my attention to him. He looked like he was trying to reach for something. "Fuck-nigga, oh no you don't. Sit yo' ass back." I crouched down to check his waist to ensure he wasn't strapped. I wanted to nip that shit in the bud right then and there.

"Jahmani, watch out!"

By the time I turned to see Doughboy come from under the table with a Tech in his hand, it was too late for me to react. "Bitch-ass nigga, me and Beans knocked yo' mama head off, and it was so sweet. Night-night."

"No!" Ari came from what seemed like nowhere with a black Cat .9 millimeter in her hand. Then she was aiming and pulling her trigger over and over again.

Pop. Pop. Pop. Pop. Pop. Pop.

Doughboy pulled his trigger. His bullets cut up the ceiling, putting big holes inside of it. Plaster fell on our heads. He stumbled into the wall and dropped his fully-automatic weapon.

P.T. took advantage of the distraction. He came from his waist with a .9 millimeter aimed directly at me and pulled the trigger.

Boom. Boom. Boom.

His bullets smacked into my chest and threw me back.

Chapter 3

It felt like I was being burned in multiple spots by a hot fireplace poker. P.T. turned his gun in the direction of Ari and fired.

Boom. Boom. Boom.

Ari ducked down and ran further into the kitchen. He jumped up and thought about pursuing her. Something made him turn his focus back on me, then the front window to the duplex shattered. A big, red brick flew into the wall and rolled onto the carpet. He looked in that direction and jumped back.

I aimed both Glocks and let them bitches ride like they'd been hitchhiking for two weeks.

Blocka. Blocka. Blocka. Blocka.

They jumped in my hand and stood him straight up. I watched one bullet fill him after the next. I kept finger-fucking my Glocks as if they were two pussies and it was prom night. The final bullet split his forehead fifty-fifty. He fell to his knees, then to his chest.

Doughboy groaned and crawled across the floor. Blood dripped out of his mouth. "Uh. Uh. Uh." He stopped and turned over.

I made it to my feet with my chest on fire. Thank God for the bullet-proof vest. I stepped over him and pulled the trigger twice. Two slugs ripped his head apart and sent him to hell.

"Ari! Ari! Which room? Which room is Lonnie in?"

Ari came back into the living room, gritting her teeth and holding her side. Blood seeped through her fingers. She pointed. "That one right there. She's in there. I feel dizzy, Jahmani." She fell to her ass and closed her eyes. "It hurt so bad. Jahmani, it hurt so bad."

I wanted to rush to her side, but I had to get to Lonnie. I had to rescue her. I made it to the closed door in the middle of the short hallway. Once there, I took a step back and kicked it as hard as I could right by the knob. The door frame splintered inward and the door burst open.

As soon as it fell away, there was Lonnie. She was lying on a dirty mattress on her back with her eyes closed, naked, her hair disheveled. Her wrists were duct taped. Between her little thighs appeared to be blood. My heart sank into my chest.

"Lonnie! Lonnie, baby. Aw, shit," I hollered and picked her up. "Baby. Baby. Wake up." She was unmoving and unresponsive to my orders. I ripped the filthy sheet from the bed and wrapped it around her, then ran back into the hallway with her. "Ari! Ari! We gotta get out of here."

Ari was laid out in the living room floor, bleeding from her stomach. She opened her eyes slightly and groaned. "Go on without me, Jahmani. I'm not gon' make it. That fool P.T. shot me, son. He got me." She closed her eyes and fainted.

Misty shocked the shit out of me. She climbed through the front room window with my .45 in her hand. "Jahmani. Jahmani. I couldn't leave you, baby. They gon' have to kill me, too. If you go, I go." When she stepped all the way inside the house and saw the scene, her eyes got big. "Oh my God. Fuck. We gotta get out of here."

I rushed over with Lonnie in my arms. "Take her back outside with you. I'ma grab Ari and follow right behind."

"Ari?" She winced. "Fuck her. We got Lonnie, now let's be on our way. It's not safe. I think I hear sirens." She took Lonnie and rushed to the back of the house, the way I'd come in. "Let's go, Jahmani!"

"Shawty, just get the Jeep ready. Do like I said!" I snapped, feeling weaker.

"Okay!" She ran out the backdoor.

I scooped Ari into my arms. As I was lifting her, she winced in pain and opened her eyes. "Jahmani, what are you doing? Put me down." She started to cry and passed back out. I was on my way out the back door when it hit me. I set Ari on the floor, grabbed a garbage bag from the bottom of the garbage, and filled it with all of the work P.T. and Doughboy had been putting together. I checked their pockets and dumped their bundles of cash and jewelry inside the bag before scooping Ari again. Then I ran out the back door with her.

***

Misty paced back and forth with her fists balled up. It was the next morning, and we were sitting inside a hospital waiting room in Greenville, North Carolina where Misty's aunt Vicki was the head doctor.

From what Misty was telling me, Vicki was born and raised in the Bronx. She'd left when she was seventeen years old after being adopted by a rich white family. Her mother and father were arrested for multiple bank robberies back in the day. Misty had called her and told her our circumstances, and she agreed to let us come and stay with her for a month with no questions asked. In my opinion, a month was all I would need to be back on my feet.

Misty shook her head. "This some bullshit, Jahmani, and you know it. You was supposed to let that bitch die. I don't give a fuck what she did in there. It's all by design. Can't nobody tell me different. Damn, this bitch just won't go away." She punched her fist into her hand.

I sat back, rubbing the bruises on my chest the vest had caused. I didn't feel like going back and forth with Misty. It seemed like no matter what I said, she found a way to attack it. "Shawty, sit yo' ass down and be cool. You working my nerves right now. I still don't know if my niece is good yet. Can't believe them sick muthafuckas was on that bullshit wit' her. She's just a baby." The thought if a grown man getting on top if my niece and forcing himself in her was causing my vision to become blurry with anger and rage.

Misty stopped and faced me. "Do this mean y'all finna get back together? Huh? Do this mean you finna kick me to the curb all because this bitch supposedly saved your life? Huh, daddy?"

I lowered my head, irritated. "Misty, sit yo' ass down before I spank you right here and right the fuck now, shawty. You driving me crazy. I ain't thinking about fucking wit' nobody right now. I'm thinking about Lonnie. I'm concerned about only my niece. Damn."

Misty mugged me. She crossed her arms in front of her chest and smacked her lips. "Oh, really? So, you mean after I just risked my life for you, the only person in this whole equation you can think about is Lonnie? I mean, it's understandable to a certain degree, but still. I thought we was in this shit together. Had I known we weren't, I definitely would've acted differently." She rolled her eyes.

That did it. I seen what I had to do. I was glad we were the only people inside the waiting room. I closed the distance between us and snatched her li'l pretty ass up, turned her back to me, and placed my hand over mouth. I carried her into the bathroom, got inside, and kicked the door closed. I dropped her to the floor and locked the door.

She bounced up with eyes wide open. "I'm sorry, daddy. I didn't mean to get on your nerves. I'm just worried you're going to–"

I grabbed her to me and sat on the single toilet in the bathroom, unbuckled her belt, and yanked her pants down along with her panties. As soon as they were to her ankles, she was over my lap, trapped. I stuffed the panties into her mouth. "Shawty, you bet not do none of that screaming shit. You make the security come in this muthafucka and I'ma body yo' li'l yellow ass. That's on my mother. Word. Lay yo' ass down."

She complied, whimpering into the panties. Her hand gripped my right ankle.

I raised my hand in the air and brought it down hard. *Smack.* She jerked upward and screamed into the panties. I smacked the other cheek just as hard. Her legs kicked and tried to break free of my hold. Then I was tearing her up with whack after whack.

"Shawty. I. Told. You. To. Sit. Yo'. Ass. Down. And. Quit. Getting. On. My. Nerves."

Whack, whack, whack.

I hit harder and harder until she was crying. Her legs opened more than once to reveal her meaty crease. The sight was tantalizing, and under different circumstances I would've had to put my dick inside her always-ready pussy, but I was too worried about Lonnie to focus on smashing Misty. I also was unsure how I was going to proceed with Ari, Linx, and Bean's bitch-ass.

She fell to the ground. She pulled the panties out of her mouth and rubbed her ass cheeks after standing up in front of me.

"Daddy, I'm sorry. I'll be better, I swear. You'll see." She climbed on my lap and wrapped her arms around my neck, kissed my lips, then rested her face in the crux of my neck. Her tongue traced up and down my skin, causing my dick to harden. She felt it and readjusted herself. "Daddy, every time you spank me, you make me yearn for you even more. I know you're angry right now, but can I please sit on it? I'm so wet, daddy. Look."

She slid her fingers between her legs and rubbed them on my lips. Her scent was alluring. Without even knowing I was doing it; I sucked her juices off her fingers and pulled her to me. My pants fell, and then she straddled my lap and positioned herself to receive me. The head of my dick separated her folds and slowly slid into her wetness.

"Uh, daddy. You're in me again." She arched her back and humped forward, arched back and humped me again, then she was riding me without inhibitions. She held my shoulders and went to work. "Un. Un. Un. Daddy. Daddy. Daddy. Yes. Fuck me. Fuck me. Fuck me. You're mine. Shit."

Her small hips rotated in a circle. I held on to her fat ass, and every time she came forward, I forced her to take all of me. She was as hot as a furnace turned all the way up and as soft as the petals of a rose. The toilet shook and sounded as if it was about to come unhinged.

She fucked me faster and faster, her mouth wide open. "Yes. Yes. Daddy. Daddy."

I didn't want to think. Her pussy was so good. I didn't want to think about why we were at the hospital or how I'd recovered Lonnie. For the moment I only wanted to focus on getting my nut. Spanking Misty had riled me up as well. Every time I spanked her thick ass, it got me heated.

She bounced higher and higher, throwing her head back. Her long, curly hair was all over her face. Her eyelids were closed tight.

"Uh. Uh. Daddy!" Now she was bucking so fast her hips were a blur. She bit into my neck and came hard, collapsed against me, breathing hard.

I picked her up and worked her hips. I was close to coming. I needed to cum in that pussy. I squeezed that juicy ass and sucked her neck. Growling and gritting my teeth, I came hard. I had a thang for her li'l ass. She was growing on me more and more. It didn't help that her pussy was so good, either.

***

Vicki smiled weakly as she stood over Lonnie's hospital bed. "This child is a fighter, that's for sure. She's been through a lot, some things so deplorable I don't even want to say out loud, but I've taken the time to record them for you to go over at your earliest convenience, and I'm quite sure you will as soon as you can. However, I just want to let you know that, by rule, I am supposed to report this ordeal. If I don't, this could cost me my license. I am in a dilemma because, while I do understand what took place, rules are rules. I haven't decided which way I'll go as of yet, but I will let you know as soon as I come to that conclusion. In regard to your friend Ari, she's already spoken with one of my good friends, who is a patrolman in the area. We'll find a way to tie both cases together and sweep them under the rug. Consider yourselves blessed." She overlooked Lonnie again. "Po' baby. Soon as she gets out of this bed, y'all bring her right on home so I can give this chil' a good home cooked meal." She leaned down and kissed her on the forehead before stepping from the room.

Misty stood up and closed the door. "Did you just hear her say Ari is in there talking to some freaking patrolman?"

I nodded and stepped beside Lonnie's bed. I rubbed the side of her cheek, then kissed it. "Yeah, I heard her."

"And that doesn't make you worried?" She looked up at me, confused.

I shook my head. "We both got bodies on our hands, shawty. I smoked a nigga, but she did, too. What she gon' say negative about me that wouldn't incriminate herself?"

Misty frowned. "I don't know, but nothing she does sit right wit' me. I am watching her ass closely. That bitch ain't finna be our downfall. Never that." She stepped around the bed and slid her arm across the small of my back. "I'm riding for you, Jahmani. You gon' see real soon just how stomp-down I really am for you."

The door opened and Ari stood in the doorway holding onto a stand that held her IV. She mugged Misty first, then myself. "While I'm in there being grilled and going through hell, this is where you are? Really?"

Chapter 4

Ari took one light step after the next until she was fully in the room. She looked into my face with a menacing glare. "Well, aren't you gonna say nothin'?"

Misty casually walked to the right side of Ari and sucked her teeth. "I don't care what you did for him back there. It ain't gon' break up what we got going on. I ain't goin', point-blank, period." Misty flared her nostrils.

Ari frowned, pushed the IV cart slightly to the side, and stepped into her face. "Bitch, you already know I'll get all in yo' ass like a wedgie. Now, I don't know what the fuck going through your mind right now, but ain't no baseball bats up in here. I'll fuck you up and then bring a few of these doctors in here to tend to yo' yellow ass. Jahmani is my man, not yours. I just saved his life, and he in turn saved mine. That's an unbreakable bond right there, side bitch!"

"Side bitch?" Misty pushed Ari out if her face and tossed her guards up. "I got yo' side bitch right here." She bounced up and down on her toes.

Ari looked as if she felt dizzy. She staggered to the wall and held herself up by it before hunching over. Then she dropped to one knee. "Bitch, I'ma get yo' ass. As soon as I'm strong enough, I'ma take a good look at you. Jahmani, call the nurse. Something ain't right."

I could see her face was turning colors. I rushed to her side and knelt down. "Ari, what's the matter?"

She shook her head and held her side. "I don't know, but I don't feel right. I feel dizzy. I feel sick. Please get the nurse, right now." She started to shake and then fell face first in the middle of the floor.

I jumped up and rushed to the nurses' station. "Look, there is a female that passed out in my niece's room. Y'all gotta come and help her ASAP," I urged.

The nurses shot up and rushed to the hospital room where they wound up scooping Ari onto a stretcher and taking her away.

As soon as they exited the room, Misty screamed in frustration. "That bitch get under my skin more than a tick would. I hate that scheming, conniving broad. I'm letting you know right now, Jahmani, she ain't coming to stay wit' us at my Aunt Vicki's. I know you still got a thing for her or whatever, but ain't no way I'ma be able to close my eyes knowing she walking around in the same household as us or sleeping under the same roof. That ain't happening. We need to find a way to get as far from New York as possible, and her. So, I'm asking you right now, please don't force me to allow this bitch to come stay wit' us." She stood patiently awaiting my response.

I shrugged my shoulders. "Shawty, that's your aunty crib. I can't impose nothing on you or her that y'all ain't trying to rock, nah mean? I'll put shawty up in a telly or somethin' until she can figure out her situation. I still need to pick her brain so I can find this nigga Beans. Ain't no way I'm finna let that chump skate after what he did to Lonnie. He ruined by niece forever wit' his sick-ass."

Misty nodded and covered her mouth, then she pointed past my shoulder. "Daddy, Lonnie waking up."

Those were some of the greatest words I'd heard in all of my life. I spun and made my way to Lonnie's side, brushing her hair out of her small face. "Princess, you woke?"

She yawned and stretched her little arms over her head, smacking her lips together before her eyes came into focus on me. "Jahmani? Uncle Jahmani." She started crying right away. "They hurt me, Uncle. They hurt me so bad." She opened her arms for me.

I hugged her small frame and kissed her soft, warm cheek. "I know they hurt you, baby. I know they did, but I'm here now, and I ain't gon' let nobody else hurt you ever again. I promise, baby. You hear me? I'm sorry I wasn't there, but I got you from here on out. I promise." My throat felt like it had a lump inside of it.

Lonnie nodded. "Okay, Uncle." She broke into a fit of sobs. "Where is my mama? I want my mama."

Damn, I didn't know what to tell her. That last I'd heard, Samantha was on the run and Dyse Avenue crew was looking for her after she was accused of setting up one of their hustlers. I didn't know if she was alive or dead, or maybe even locked up by now. I would have to do my research after I left the hospital, I thought. "As soon as you're all better, we're going to find her. I don't know where she is right now, but she loves you, and she told me to make sure you safe and sound. So, I'm going to take good care of you until she comes back, okay?"

Lonnie sat up. She looked panicked. "But what if Beans come back?" She started to shake real bad. "He said if I told on him, he was going to kill me and hurt my mom real bad. He showed me a gun. What if he hurt her already? It's all my fault. I shouldn't've told the nurse lady what happened to me. But I was so scared."

Misty climbed into the bed with Lonnie and pulled her into her arms. "Oh, baby." There were tears in Misty's eyes. "You don't have to worry about Beans no more. We're not even in New York City any longer. We're a long way from there. Beans doesn't have a clue where we are. Neither does anybody else that has hurt you. You are perfectly safe, and me and your uncle Jahmani are going to see to it that those bad guys stay away from you forever." She hugged her tighter and kissed her forehead.

I was so heated that my eyes watered. I couldn't believe

any grown-ass nigga would hurt a child the way Beans had. I had to have his ass. That was a form of beef I would never be able to let go. I mean, I was vexed over what they'd done to my mother, but Lonnie's ordeal had me seeing stars, I was so mad.

I scooted to the other side if the bed and wrapped my free arm around her neck. "I got you, princess. You're good. Your uncle ain't going nowhere."

"Neither is your Aunty Misty. I'm right here. You are safe," Misty cooed.

***

Vicki kept Lonnie under watch for four days total, then released her to me. For some reason Ari continued to have complications, so Vicki ordered she remain in the hospital for an additional week so they could run some tests and monitor her. This last bit of news made Misty happy. She had a big smile on her face as we rolled Lonnie to the front door of the hospital in a wheelchair. When we got to the parking lot, I helped her get into the back seat of Vicki's Lincoln Navigator and strapped her in.

Misty got behind the steering wheel and blew a kiss at me as she pulled out of the parking lot. She adjusted her rearview mirror and sighed. "You think she gon' be okay?"

It was a bright and sunny day. The sun shone high in the sky. I rolled down my window a bit so I could catch a whiff of the breeze that was flowing through. The air smelled different than that of New York City, almost foreign. "Lonnie got my blood in her. Of course she gon' be okay. We just gotta take it one day at a time. It'll be a while, but in the end she'll prevail."

Misty looked her over again. "She's very beautiful, though. I can see why you're so crazy about her. What's good with her mother?"

"I don't know. Shawty be all over the place. I know she was beefing wit' them Dyse Avenue kats real tough. Then she got in some law issues like myself, but just like my niece, she's a real tough chick, too. I'ma find her soon, but right now my main priority is getting this baby to a safe haven."

Misty reached and squeezed my thigh. "Jahmani, I don't know Lonnie just yet, but I'm letting you know right now I love her because I love you. Whenever you're not around, I'm going to make sure she is always more than taken care of. I got your back. I'ma show you what I mean." She continued to drive.

I turned all the way around and looked my niece over. As soon as Lonnie smiled at me, I felt my heart skip a beat. I was insane over her. "I love you, li'l mama."

"I love you, too, Uncle."

After fifteen minutes of driving, Misty finally pulled up in front if Vicki's three-story home. It looked huge from the outside. It was white-bricked with a picket fence around it and a two-car garage. The lawn was mown perfectly, and the bushed was neatly trimmed. There was a sprinkler in the middle of the yard watering the grass. The grass smelled freshly cut. Vicki's home was on a block with what seemed like twenty others. Hers in particular sat at the apex of a cul-de-sac. Cars took the street all the way to the end and then had to make a U-turn in order to get out.

I stepped out of the truck and opened the back door, helping Lonnie out of her seat. She wrapped her arms around my neck and her legs around my waist. Her face rested in the crux of my neck. "I love you, Uncle."

I rubbed her back and kissed her cheek. "I love you, too."

Misty opened the door to the massive home and stepped to the side. I almost dropped Lonnie as a big-ass German

Sheppard came running from the back of the house and directly toward me. I searched my waist for a pistol I didn't have. A pistol I'd left in the truck. "Holy shit, Misty, get that muthafuckin' dog! Get him now!" I held Lonnie tighter in my arms and turned my back to the approaching canine.

Misty blocked its path immediately. "Hey, Hondo! No!" She grabbed his collar and pulled him away from us. Hondo whined and tried to break away from her. He barked and jumped up and down, whining some more before sniffing the air.

Misty dragged him to the back of the house and released him to the backyard. After the dog ran into the yard, she closed the door and washed her hands in the kitchen sink. "I'm sorry about that, daddy. I should've told you she got a dog. Boy, am I glad you didn't have your pistol on you. That would've been one dead mutt."

"You already know. Them German Sheppards in the Bronx be vicious as hell. I've seen a few of them rip the throats out of Pit bulls."

Lonnie shook in my arms. "I don't like dogs, Uncle. They're too mean."

Misty rubbed her back. "It's okay, baby. Hondo is a nice dog. He's just a big baby. He won't hurt you. You'll see. Come on, let me show you where we'll be staying." She waved for me and Lonnie to follow her.

He house was nicely furnished. When we walked through the living room, I saw there was what looked like an eighty-inch flat screened television hanging on the wall right over a fireplace. The couches were all white leather. Vicki had glass tables and paintings of abstract art that adorned the walls. Her home smelled of incense. The upkeep looked superb. I always felt I could tell a lot about a woman by the upkeep of her home, and since I believed I was already digging Vicki, I took her to be well put-together like her home. I couldn't wait until I got the chance to actually sit down and pick her brain.

We ascended the stairs and came to the second landing. As soon as we got to the top, Misty paused. "Damn, I forgot Vicki don't let nobody wear shoes in her home. We gotta take ours off before she goes crazy." She kicked off her Timbs, and so did I. Lonnie was rocking the shoes with the soft bottoms from the hospital, so she was good to go.

We walked down a long hallway that had white carpet. When we got about halfway down it, Misty came to a door and pushed it open. She stepped inside. "This is the room Lonnie will be staying in. Of course, we'll make it a li'l homier for her, but for now this is what it is."

The room was huge. There was a fifty-inch flat screen on the wall, a queen-sized bed, and a dresser. A small half-bathroom was connected to it as well.

I tried to put Lonnie down, but she clung to me, kicking her legs at the air. "No. No. No. I don't wanna stay in here by myself. Please. Beans gon' get me," she cried and looked as if she were ready to have a temper tantrum.

I picked her back up and held her close. "It's okay, baby girl. It's okay. I got you. You don't have to sleep in here right now."

Misty looked sympathetic. She covered her mouth with her right hand and shook her head from side to side. "Those bastards really hurt this baby. They should be ashamed of themselves."

"Baby, where are we sleeping?"

Misty groaned. "Aw, that's the first time you called me baby since we been doing our thing together." She hugged me and stood on her tippy-toes to kiss my cheek. "Come on, daddy." She walked out into the hallway and directly across the hall. "This is where we will be staying. It's my old room with a few new, modern additions."

Her room was huge as well. She also had a fifty-inch television mounted on the wall. In the left corner of the room was an entertainment system, and to the left of that was a massive closet. All the way to my right was a balcony that overlooked the backyard. Her room seemed very cozy. I was feeling it one hundred percent.

"What do you think, daddy?" she asked, smiling up at me.

I gazed over at the huge king-sized bed and imagined fuckin' the shit out of her in it. The headboard was all wood. There was a night table to the right of the bed with a lamp on it. There was also a little drawer on the nightstand where I imagined Misty kept her adult toys, if she had them.

"I like it. I mean, I ain't trying to be here too long, but I most definitely like what I see."

"Good, as long as you're happy."

Chapter 5

After fighting with Lonnie for four nights trying to get her to sleep in the other room on her own, I officially gave up and saw that in order for her to fall asleep each night, I would have to be beside her. So I took to reading her stories off my phone until she'd fall asleep, or I'd tell her some of the things me and her father, who was my brother Pacho, did as kids. Those old stories always seemed to make her fall asleep with a big smile on her face.

On the eighth night we were there, after I'd put Lonnie to sleep, I was making my way out of Lonnie's room when I bumped into Misty in the hallway. She stood staring at me with her pretty, light-brown eyes.

"You know, Jahmani, you're real good with Lonnie. That's a turn-on for any woman watching you in action." She stepped up to me and kissed my lips. She had on pink, laced boy shorts that were real tight on her. The material seemed to conform to her like a second skin.

My hands sailed down her round ass and cupped the cheeks. The panties were so small that most of the cheeks were hanging out of them anyway. Her skin was hot and soft. I sucked on her lips and ran my tongue all over them. "You think it's about time I hit this pussy, baby?"

She shivered. "Every time you call me baby, it does something to me. And hell yeah, I'm fien'ing for you, Jahmani. I wish you could fuck me right here in this hallway. I don't care if my aunt catches us." She slid her hand into my pajama pants and squeezed my dick. It grew in her hand at the mentioning of her aunt catching us. I was all for that forbidden shit. Besides, Vicki was an older woman, but fine as Heaven.

I held her against the wall and dropped down. It was one-something in the morning, and the house was quiet. I could hear crickets making their sounds. I placed my nose right on Misty's sex lips and sniffed them through her panties. She smelled like perfume down there, and while it was a welcoming scent, I wanted to smell her pussy. I stuck my nose all the way into her crack and sniffed again, rubbed the area, and sniffed harder.

She moaned, opening her thick golden thighs. "Daddy, what are you trying to do to me?" Her hands cupped her C-cup titties. Her hard nipples poked through the pink beater. She pulled on them and jerked into my face.

I pulled her crotch band to the side. One yellow lip exposed itself. I flicked it with my tongue, sucked on it, and flicked it some more. I yanked the material all the way to the left and revealed her entire meaty, bald pussy. The sight excited me. She spread her thick-ass thighs further apart. My tongue traveled up and down her slit while my nose rubbed against her clitoris.

"Mm. Mm. Daddy. Eat me. Please eat your baby." Misty licked all over her lips.

I slid two fingers into her box and worked them in and out, pulled them to my mouth, and sucked them clean before inserting them back inside of her. Then they were fingering her at full speed while my lips trapped her pearl and sucked hard on it.

She held my head by the sides, humping my face. Now I was getting the full scent of her pussy. It was driving me crazy.

"Uh. Uh. Daddy. You finna make me. Uh." She humped faster and faster.

I placed her thigh on my shoulder and attacked that pussy with no remorse. My tongue took on a mind of its own. It ran circles around her digit. I slurped her juices and held her tight.

She screamed and came in my face, her pussy skeeting at me. "Huh. Huh. Huh. Un, shit, daddy." Her knees got weak.

She fell against me.

I turned her around and kissed all over that fat ass. When a female was as thick as she was, they deserved to have that ass kissed and worshipped for the greater good of humanity. I sucked hickeys all over it and even took my time to trace circles around her anus. Misty slid her fingers between her thighs and pinched her clit. I watched her play with her pussy while she moaned. My dick was so hard it felt like it was about to pop off.

"Take me in the room, daddy. Take me in there and fuck me good." She turned around and took ahold of my pipe, stroking it.

Vicki opened her bedroom door and caught us in the act. She stepped into the hallway with a short, purple negligee on. Her cropped, curly hair fell over her high cheekbones. The negligee was short enough to reveal her own set of hefty golden thighs.

She placed her hand on her hip. "Uh-uh. I gave y'all a whole-ass room to do y'all thang in, yet I find y'all in my hallway turning it into a porno set?" She shook her head.

Her titties looked to be every bit of a D-cup. The areola was prominent against the material. This made my dick jump even higher. Misty took her hand off of my pipe, exposing it to her aunt's gaze. She must've realized what she'd done, and her eyes got big and then she stood in front of me, shielding he from Vicki's hungry glare.

"I'm sorry, Vicki. We'll finish this off in here. Come on, Jahmani." Misty grabbed ahold of my knob and pulled me into the room behind her.

Before we cleared the doorjamb, Vicki and I made eye contact. She licked her sexy lips and smiled at me.

Misty closed the door and pushed me up against it. She dropped to her knees and stroked my piece. "She seen it, baby.

Vicki seen what you working wit', and that's driving me crazy. I don't know why." She sucked me into her mouth and slurped me back and forth with blazing speed, rubbing all over my abs.

I closed my eyes and enjoyed her head game. Slowly, on their own accord, my hips began to rock back and forth. I fucked her face and stepped away from her, pulling by pajama pants all the way down and off and stroking my piece. "I want yo' li'l thick-ass from the back. Bend over that bed, my bitch. Hurry up." I grabbed a handful of her hair to assist her in getting into position.

She groaned and bent over the bed, spread her feet, and looked back at me with her bottom lip trembling. "Daddy, I need you. I need to know I belong to you. Tell me that while you fuck me."

I placed the head on the center of her pussy lips and pushed inward. Her lips opened and invited me into her hot, moist treasures. The heat was unbelievable. Her moisture leaked out of her and ran down her thighs. I slid halfway in, then slammed forward.

"Uh! Daddy!" She licked her bottom lip.

I grabbed ahold of her hips and started to beat that pussy in from the back. *Smack. Smack. Smack. Smack. Smack. Smack. Smack. Smack. Smack.* Faster and harder.

"Un. Un. Un. Daddy. Daddy. Uh. Uh. Yes! Yes. Yes. Aw, shit. Fuck me." She bounced back into my lap. Her back arched. Her fists were balled in the sheets from the bed.

I rubbed all over that yellow moon, slapped her backside, and dove deeper and deeper. More than once my eyes rolled into the back of my head. The scent of her pussy was sending me on a journey all on its own. "Misty. Misty. Fuck, baby. Fuck, ma. This. Pussy. So. Good. Fuck. Uh," I groaned, stroking her faster and faster.

Her fist beat on the mattress now. She clenched her teeth,

moaning loudly. She tried her best to look back at me. Her right breast had worked its way out of her tank top. The baby bottle-sized nipple was erect and looked succulent. "I'm. Finna. Cum. Daddy. Aw. Daddy. Shit. I'm cumming!" She grabbed a pillow and screamed into it, starting to shake like crazy, and fell on her stomach.

I grabbed her right ankle and held it up while my dick continued to plunge away in her garden. Her pussy was super sloppy-wet. I could hear the sounds as we did our thing. She arched her back all the way and placed her head right under my nose. I caught a whiff of her shampoo and conditioner, and for some reason the girly scent set me off. I began to cum hard. "Uh. Uh. Shit. Baby. Mm. Mm. Uh."

***

After our fuck session, Misty dipped off to use the bathroom. When she came back, she slipped into the bed beside me, took ahold of my piece, and sucked it into her mouth. After cleansing me of our fluids, she climbed up my body and laid her head on my chest.

"Jahmani, I need you to know that I love you, and I will do anything for you. Do you believe that?"

Her body felt good lying beside mine. I pulled her up so she was on top of me. Once there, I gripped her naked backside. "Actions speak louder than words, shawty. You can tell me anything when we're in a safe haven like this, but when the shit hits the fan, it can be a whole other story. Far as that love shit you spitting at me, how can you say you love me already, and we still getting to know each other? What have I done to make you love me?"

Misty straddled me and sat up. She looked so sexy, looking into my eyes the way she was doing, that I felt myself getting aroused again. She had to be one of the baddest redbones I had ever seen in my life, and I was from the Bronx. Most of the women in the Bronx were bad because they were mixed with so many different races, yet Misty was ridiculously gorgeous.

"Jahmani, I can't really explain how it is I know I love you, but I know I do. I fell in love with you at first sight. Then, after getting to know you, I fell in love with your struggles and your dominant personality. You're one-of-a-kind, and your heart is so pure. I mean, look at the extremes you were willing to go to for Lonnie. It says a lot about a man's character anytime he is willing to risk his life for somebody else's. That's admirable. Your sex game also helps," she giggled. "As far as when the shit hits the fan and how I'll be, well, I'm sure you saw that. I busted out a window to cause a distraction. I knew you were going to pop some shit up when I did that, and I knew it would distract the enemy long enough for you to get an upper hand. Either way, I was coming through that window for my man. For my daddy. So don't flex on me like you don't know I'm 'bout that muthafuckin' life when it comes to you. Because I am." She slapped my chest and frowned. "Nigga, you hear me?"

I laughed. "Yeah, baby, I hear you."

She shook her head. "Wait a minute, let me rephrase that question. Nigga, do you believe me?"

I rubbed all over that juicy booty. "Yeah, daddy believe you. I know you'da bust that thang for me. I'ma have to show you how to use it, though, ain't I?" I pulled her down to me. I wanted to feel her soft titties against my chest.

"I ain't never shot one before, but I'm willing to learn, daddy, so when the shit does hit the fan, I'll be able to wipe it up with my own version of tissue. I just wanna ride for you in every single way I can."

I pulled her blouse over her head and made her lay back on

top of me. "Shawty, on some real shit, you wanna know something?"

She nodded. "What's that, daddy?"

"I care about you, girl. I don't understand how you're growing on me so quick, but I'm most definitely falling for you. I gotta keep you by my side. You make me feel some type of way every time you're near me. That shit ain't normal for me. I ain't used to falling for nobody. It's hard for me to develop feelings because I don't trust nobody."

Misty looked up into my eyes and rubbed my chest. "You can trust me, daddy. I am the one person that will never betray you. I'll stand by your side, ten toes down through the fire and until my last breath. I promise you this on my soul."

She kissed my lips again. That was another thing about Misty. She was so affectionate that it was hard to not fall hard for her. She was always rubbing, kissing, or hugging me. She was like my own personal leech that at first got on my nerves, but now it was like I was falling in love with those characteristics.

"I'ma hold you to that, baby. But for tonight, be quiet and just be my li'l teddy bear. Let's get some sleep." I opened her legs and slid my piece back into her, and we fell asleep just like that.

Ghost

Chapter 6

It was two weeks after we'd gotten to North Carolina before Ari was finally released from the hospital. I wheeled her out the doors and we jumped into the Buick Lacrosse Vicki had allowed me to roll around the city in. Ari pulled her seatbelt across her chest and clicked it into place. "Yo, I hope you don't think I'm about to go and lay up in the same fuckin' house as this bitch when she dirty-macked you from me. If you think that's the case, you got another thing coming." She pulled down the sun visor to block the rays of the sun.

I pulled out of the lot and made a right into the busy intersection. I was able to roll for a minute before I stopped at the red light. "Ari, I know you and shawty beefing. I would never ask you to stay under the same roof as her. I don't feel like all of that drama and shit, no way. Now, as far as her dirty-macking me, shawty, I'm a grown-ass man. Can't nobody force me to do shit I don't want to do. I was feeling her just as hard as she was feeling me. Besides, you was all up that nigga P.T.'s ass, anyway."

"Jahmani, I swear to God, you better stop playin' wit' me. You already know I was going through it. After I saw our pictures in the news talking about us being murders, I freaked all the way out. I needed to be away from you for a little while. P.T. was familiar. Luckily I did choose to go back and fuck wit' him. Had I not, I would have never been able to find Lonnie for you. By the way, you still haven't thanked me for that. Are you waiting on a special occasion, or?"

I laughed at that. "Yo, thank you, shawty. Word is bond, had you never did what you did, I wouldn't have my niece right now. I owe you like a muthafucka."

Ari scoffed. "Could've fooled me. I been in that hospital for two weeks. I ain't seen yo' ass since you left wit' Lonnie and Misty. That was cold, how you did me, and after I got shot saving yo' life." She lowered her head, then looked out the window.

I sighed dejectedly. She was right. I was bogus as hell. Had she not smoked Dough Boy, he would've killed me for sure. She was also responsible for saving Lonnie's life, as well. I should've been by her side the entire time she was in the hospital. I was real foul for not being there. "I'm sorry, Ari. You are absolutely right. I should've had your back, and I didn't. I been so focused on getting Lonnie up to par that I forgot about you in the process. I should've been better."

"I don't think it had much to do wit' Lonnie and more so everything to do wit' Misty. You stuck on her red-ass. I still can't believe you fucking my cousin, Jahmani. Damn you. How you just gon' give up on me like that? You did all that fuckin' sweating me stuff, then soon as things get heavy you jump to my cousin. You niggas all the same. Damn, I hate you at times." She rolled down her window and rested her arm on the windowsill.

"Ari, I don't know what to say about that. You was gone for however many days, and I was sure you was fuckin' wit' some other nigga, so I got at shawty. It is what it is. Life goes on."

She adjusted in her seat. "What's that supposed to mean? You saying y'all are an item now? That's who you gon' be with from here on out?"

"I'm being wit' myself. I ain't wit' nobody. It's too much going on for me to be thinking about perfecting a fuckin' relationship. Shawty, if you was that worried about that, you should've never left when you did. How I'm supposed to react to you laying up with some other nigga? That simp shit ain't in me, li'l one. Then when I come over there to get you, expressing my feelings and all that shit, you snub me for that chump. Bitch, miss me wit' that you-fucking-my-cousin shit. It is what it is."

She sat quietly, clenching her jaw. Her face turned into a frown. The sunlight reflected off her forehead. "You so stupid you still don't see why I did all this P.T. shit, do you? You got your fuckin' niece back, and you still don't see why I did what I did! You killed my fuckin' brother, Jahmani. My brother and my cousin, and I'm still riding for your cold-hearted ass, but you don't get it. Pull this fuckin' car over! Now!" she screamed.

I kept rolling because I was still trying to mentally process everything. The fact she was getting frustrated caused my temper to rise. I tried to see things logically, but no matter which angle I came from within the recesses of my mind, I felt like Ari was blowing smoke. Her stumbling upon Lonnie during her laying up with P.T. seemed like happenstance.

"Jahmani, I said pull this fuckin' car over. Now!"

I drove about half a block and pulled the whip over to the curb. Before it came to a halt, she jumped out of it and slammed the door so hard it cracked the window she'd partially rolled back up.

She mugged me through the fractured glass. "As smart as yo' black ass is, you ain't nothing but a fuckin' simpleton! You got yo' head so far up that yellow bitch's ass that you can see what she ate yesterday. I took a bullet for you, Jahmani. I rearranged by whole life for your no-good ass, and this is how you repay me?" She waved me off and proceeded to storm down the sunny street, holding her side. She walked gingerly. I could tell she was still in some form of pain.

I jumped out of the whip and took off after her. When I caught up to her, I grabbed her arm and held her in place. "Ari, wait a minute. Where the fuck are you going?"

She pulled away from me and winced in pain, hugging

herself. "Don't worry about it, Jahmani. You don't give a damn, anyway. All you care about is Misty and Lonnie. Well, I'm not going to be your fuckin' afterthought. I deserve more than that. You're not going to make me some vulnerable basket case. You're not going to continue to pull me down. I can do bad all by myself." She turned to walk away from me again.

It felt like it was getting hotter outside. The humidity was most definitely making its presence felt, which was crazy because only a few weeks prior New York had felt like the South Pole to me.

I stood there for a moment, feeling stubborn. I was seconds away from saying 'fuck her' and allowing her to go wherever she wanted to. I wanted to wash my hands of her and just be done, but she stepped off the curb and began to walk across the busy street without caution. Cars slammed on their brakes while others blew their horns at her. She seemed to pay them no mind and continued to cross the street. She stopped in the middle of it with cars whizzing by her and held her arms out at her sides.

"I'm pregnant with your child, Jahmani. You wanna know why they kept me in that hospital longer than Lonnie? It's because the bullet I took for yo' ass almost hurt our child. But you don't give a fuck, now do you?" She turned to walk away again. Now cars were beeping their horns at her, rolling down their windows and calling her all kinds of bitch in their southern drawls before storming away again.

I tried to make my way through the traffic. My heart sunk into my stomach. Pregnant? How the fuck could she be pregnant? And if she was, how could she for sure know it was by me? She'd been with P.T. as well. I was sure they'd gotten down while her and I had been together. I wasn't falling for that Boo Boo the Fool stunt.

"Yo, Ari! Ari! Hold up, shawty!" I waited until a city bus passed by and jogged across the street after her.

She waved me off again and started to run down the residential block after she'd cleared the busy street. I jogged behind her, irritated. It was hot. I'd left Vicki's car running, and I didn't know nothing about Greenville. I already felt out-of-bounds, so when I caught up to her this time, I was more aggressive. I took ahold of her arm and pulled her to me.

"Shawty, what the fuck is your problem? Why you acting all stupid and shit? I thought you was more mature than this."

She looked up at me with her forehead sweating. It slid down the side of her face. Then she yanked her arm away again. "That's what you have to say to me after I just told you what it was? Nigga, get off of me!" She wiped her forehead free of sweat. "Jahmani, I swear, I wish I'd never gotten involved with your ass. I wish I'd never allowed those smooth words to win me over. When you showed up at my pad in the Bronx all messed up, I should've allowed you to die. You ain't been nothing but one portion of intense pain after the next. I swear to God, I hate you right now, and if it's the last thing I do, I'ma get you to feel the way I feel right in this moment." She went and sat on somebody's porch with her head down.

Damn, I didn't know why, but I felt like shit. I'd never seen Ari act so discombobulated. She seemed lost, as if her heart was broken. I didn't even think she cared about our relationship this much. She was most definitely throwing me for a loop.

I sat beside her and maintained my silence. Reaching out, I rubbed her back. She arched away from it and stood up.

"Don't fuckin' touch me." She took a deep breath and shook her head. "I need to know what we're going to do, Jahmani. We're both on the run, and I'm pregnant. You're living in some freaking house, shacked up with my cousin, and

I'm pregnant. I'm way the hell out here in North Carolina without a pot to piss in, and I'm pregnant. We don't know which way is up or down, oh, and might I remind you that I'm pregnant with your child? What are we going to do? What?" Now she was pacing back and forth again.

I stood up and took ahold of her shoulders. "Ari, calm down. Damn. You're only getting yourself riled up for no reason. We'll figure this out together. First thing we gotta do is get you a room so you can get some rest. You need to chill for a few weeks. I'll take care of you, and then we'll figure out our next move."

"You'll take care of me? Really? Yeah, well, I already see where you taking care of me has gotten me so far. Pregnant, addicted to dope, and mourning the loss of my fuckin' brother. You taking care of me is not something I can ease into the thought of. I mean, let's just be honest." She ran her fingers through her hair. "Besides, I'm a grown-ass woman. I can take care of myself just fine. I been doing it all of these years so far." She stepped past me and took off back in the direction we'd come from.

"Where the fuck are you going now?" I hollered, getting vexed.

"Back to the damn car. I ain't got no money, and I do need to lay my ass down. You finna book me into a nice, luxurious hotel so I can kick back. Don't think you finna put me in a motel, either, nigga. I definitely ain't going. Come on!" she hollered, wiping sweat from her pretty face again and holding her side.

As much as I wanted to snap out on her ass, I felt like there was a time and a place for everything. I wanted to get to the bottom of this whole pregnancy thing and find out if she was really carrying my seed or not. If she was, that would cause one hell of a dilemma. There was no way I was going to leave her out on a limb if she had my kid. Second to that, a child meant smarter survival. It meant I had to get my chips up. It also meant I had to find a way to come out from under the heat I was under. I was a wanted man, not just by the authorities, but by the animals in the slums of New York as well. Not to mention I was feeling crazy hatred toward Beans and his whole setup. Them niggas had to pay for what they'd done to Lonnie and my mother. There was no way around that.

***

I booked Ari into the Hilton Luxurious Grand Hotel and paid up her bill for a month. That shit put a major dent in my pocket, but if she was carrying my seed, that was the way things were supposed to go. I didn't want to get to the bottom of it on the first night. It seemed every time I approached the situation, we wound up falling out. That shit got old quick, so I wound up making sure she put something on her stomach, changed her old bandages, and putting new ones on for her before I got ready to head out for the night. As I turned the knob to pull the door open, she stopped me.

"Jahmani."

I turned around to see her sitting on the edge of the bed with her head down. "What's good, Ari?"

She was quiet for a moment, rubbing her hands together, then sighed. "I don't want to be alone tonight. I mean, I know you're in a rush to get back to her and everything, and that's cool, but I'm in a new city. I don't know anybody, and this is my first day out of the hospital. I just don't feel like being alone." She kept her head hung.

"You don't have to be. Shawty, I wish you would stop fighting me so much and just talk to me. I'm not the enemy. We're supposed to be in this shit together."

"How can we be when you're on your way back to my cousin? You got me feeling so low right now. It's not right, and you know it's not. Now, I don't want to be alone, and you bet not leave, but I don't want you to say a word to me. My mind is all screwed up right now." She climbed into the bed and pulled the covers back, stripped down to her bikini panties, and slid under the blankets, lying on her side. "Get up here and hold me, Jahmani. You owe me at least that."

She glared at me until I slid behind her. Once she was scooted back to my chest, she closed her eyes.

"Ari, on everythang, you the only person can talk to me as snobby as you do and still get your way. I wouldn't accept that from nobody else." I wanted to make sure she knew that.

"Jahmani, I said I didn't want you to say another word to me. Just hold me, and we'll talk about everything in the morning, Lord willing. Goodnight." She turned out the lamp and snuggled against my chest.

"You know I can't sleep here tonight. I have to get back to Lonnie. I can hold you 'til you fall asleep, though."

"I guess that's cool. It's better than nothing," she huffed.

Chapter 7

I fell asleep that night and didn't leave the hotel until late the next afternoon. Even though I stayed that long, Ari still refused to discuss anything with me that mattered. It had turned out to be a complete waste of time. When I told her I had to go and check on Lonnie, she flipped out, slapping me across the face before pushing me into the hallway and slamming the door. She was testing my patience, and I didn't know how much longer I was going to allow her to do such.

When I pulled up to Vicki's crib at about two o'clock the next afternoon, Misty was waiting on the porch, sitting in a rocking chair in a colorful sundress that made her look like she was one of the locals. She didn't even wait for me to pull into the driveway good enough before she was running up to the car.

She slammed her hand on the hood. "Where you been, Jahmani? Huh? Where the fuck you been, daddy?"

I stepped out of the car and walked past her ass. I was done arguing with females for the day, at least that was how I felt. My patience had run thinner than a starving model. I just wanted to see Lonnie. I needed to hold her in my arms so I could turn my cold heart a li'l warmer. "I was wit' Ari. Shawty trying to get adjusted after being laid up in the hospital for a few weeks. That's it. I don't feel like doing all this arguing and shit." I made my way up the porch steps.

She ran ahead. "You fucked that bitch again, didn't you? You had to. Come here and let me smell your dick, Jahmani, I wanna smell it right now." She cupped my pipe and started to undo my pants.

I knocked her hands off me. "Man, g'on. Chill yo' crazy ass out. I ain't even fuck her. All she wanted me to do was hold her all night. Then, when the morning came, she was on some silent shit. I ain't wake up until about ten anyway. Move."

Misty stood there with her head down. She moved just enough for me to brush past her. As I stepped into the house, I thought she was going to follow me, but instead she took a seat on the rocking chair again.

"Yo, bring ya ass in here and let me holla at you for a minute," I ordered, standing in the doorway.

She shook her head. "Nall, you g'on 'head. I need to cool down. I'll be in there in a minute." She picked up her phone and started to do somethin' on it that I couldn't quite tell.

I sucked my teeth and left her ass on the porch. It was too early in the day to be doing a bunch if arguing. On top of that, I was hungrier than a sumo wrestler walking into a buffet. I stepped inside the house and smelled a chili aroma that was intoxicating, and I really wasn't a chili fan.

When I saw Vicki shaking her groove thang in front of the stove, adding her li'l seasonings and nodding her head to the Keith Sweat song crooning out of the speakers, I couldn't help but feel a tad bit homesick and in need of a good meal prepared by this goddess. I didn't care if it was good or not, I just wanted to taste it. I eased into her kitchen and sniffed the air again after kicking my Airmax shoes off at the door.

"Yo, Ms. Vicki, it smell like Heaven up in here. What you cooking, goddess?"

She spun around and slid across the floor. "Somethin', somethin'. Somethin', somethin' just ain't right," she sang Keith Sweat's lyrics, smiled, and stroked my chin. Her curly hair bounced and made her look so fuckin' gorgeous. "I'm making my infamous North Carolina Ghost Pepper Chili. My son gon' be dropping by in a few hours. He coming from Baltimore, and I wanted to cook his favorite dish before he got here. Plus, you look like you can use a hearty meal yaself." She stepped back up to the stove and stirred the pot, took a handful of shredded cheese, dropped it inside, and stirred it again.

The air smelled so good that I flicked my tongue out to see if I could taste the aroma she had going all throughout the house. While she was cooking with her back turned to me, I took the time to trail my eyes down and catch a glimpse of what she was working wit' back there. She had on a pair of black biker shorts. Her ass was poked out like a pregnant belly. When she had on her doctor's uniform, I couldn't tell just how thick she was, but now I was taken aback. Vicki was strapped, and she had that sexy older woman vibe coming off of her.

"Damn, Ms. Vicki, you something else, ain't you?" My eyes never left that ass.

She looked over her shoulder and popped back on her legs. This made the shorts sink inside her rounded cheeks. "Why you say that, suga'?"

She definitely caught me peeping her because I was brazen with it. Even though I knew she was looking at me, I still didn't take my eyes off her backside.

"Nothing. Yo, make sure I get a nice bowl of whatever you whipping up. I can tell you know what you doing. Ain't no doubt about that. Damn."

She laughed. "Boy, you better go see what's the matter wit' my niece," she whispered. "She just came into the house wit' a angry scowl on her face. I ain't never seen her that red before." She pointed. "But I got you, baby. I'll make sure you're good, don't worry," she smiled.

Yo, I ain't know this queen from Adam, but I stepped forward and kissed her on the cheek. "Thank you, Miss Vicki."

While kissing her cheek, I definitely bumped up against that backside. I had to covertly see what that felt like. It was soft and full of heat. I could imagine fucking her from the back. I'd explore all types of mommy issues wit' her. Damn, she was fine.

"Don't mention it, baby. Now, g'on make sure that Misty is good."

Misty stepped into the doorway of the kitchen and crossed her arms across her chest. "Jahmani, let me holler at you outside in the back for a minute."

Before I could answer, she walked away toward the back of the house, opened the door, and wound up in the backyard. I followed her. As soon as I stepped outside, the blinding sun attacked me. I shielded my eyes from it. It cast a glow across the top of the swimming pool's blue water. Vicki had her pool equipped with a mini-slide and diving board. There were four lounge chairs set up around the pool and two umbrella tables with chairs around them. I already saw out back was where I was going to spend a lot of my time.

Misty pulled the sundress over her head and walked across the hot pavement. She wore a purple thong that separated her golden ass cheeks. She eased into a lounge chair and crossed her thick thighs, grabbed another one, and pulled it closer to her. "Come on, Jahmani, damn."

Shit, since she was shedding clothes, then I felt I might as well shed a few, too. I pulled my polo t-shirt over my head, then my black wife-beater, dropped them on a lounge chair, and took a seat beside her. "Yo, what's good wit' Lonnie?"

"She's cool. I just put her down for a nap right before you pulled up. She was asking about you. We were both worried." She took a tuft of her long, curly hair and placed it behind her ear. "What stopped you from calling me last night, Jahmani? You telling me you wasn't too busy fucking her?"

I leaned back in the chair. The sunlight shined down on my abs. I was hoping Ms. Vicki peeked outside so she could see me in all of my glory. I would give her the bitness, like, ASAP if given the chance. Couldn't help thinking about that wet pussy.

"Hello? Are you going to give me an answer, or are you too busy trying to think up a lie you think I'm going to be naïve enough to believe?"

"Baby, you wiling right now. I'm telling you, ain't nothing happen last night. I told you what it was. That's it. The reason I ain't call you is because I ain't feel like arguing or debating you on whether I should've been there to support her or not. She did save my life, and she is the main reason I got Lonnie back. Whether you wanna admit that or not, it's the truth."

Misty sucked her teeth. "How you know she ain't have nothing to do wit' her being abducted in the first place? I'm telling you, that bitch is gon' be the death of you. You don't know her like I do. She's very sneaky. Very conniving and calculating. Nothing goes on with her that she doesn't want to. It's been that way ever since we were kids. That bitch knew if she made you spend the night with her last night, it was going to cause some form of chaos between us. She probably laying back right now laughing, plotting her next move. Ugh. You fell for that shit."

"Shawty, is you more worried about what her and I was supposed to have done last night, or if I'm supposedly falling for her tactics?"

Misty looked into eyes. "Both. Look, Jahmani, I need to figure out what's about to go on with us. I know I'm young, but I ain't got no time for these mind games. I'm trying to be with you, and only you. I love you already, and I think if we can get our priorities in order, we can be something special to one another. But if that is to be the case, then we gotta be one hunnit all around the board. So, my question to you is what do you want to do when it comes to you and I?"

I watched the sun shimmer off the water in the pool. "Misty, you're my baby girl. Ain't shit finna change that.

Right now we have so many odds against us that it's crazy. I'm wanted by the law. Lonnie's mother is still missing. I gotta get up with that nigga Beans for all the shit he did to me and my people. And on top of that, I gotta get my bands up so I can support Lonnie, you, and myself. And just on some real shit, Ari, too. Shawty busted and disgusted, too, with the law bearing down on her. I gotta figure some shit out quick." I closed my eyes and enjoyed the gentle breeze that coursed through the backyard as a cloud covered the direction of the sun's rays.

Misty reached over and pinched the skin surrounding my ribs. "Nigga, you still ain't answer my fuckin' question. What are we to each other?"

I smacked her assaulting fingers off my body. That shit felt like a bee sting. I jumped up and mugged her pretty ass. "Bitch, I oughta spank yo' muthafuckin' ass for that stupid shit." I looked over the place where she'd pinched me. It was bright red.

"Well, answer my fuckin' question then. You ain't finna be stringing me along like I'm some nobody-ass bitch. If this ain't what you want, then you need to tell me this right now. You already got my heart hurting." She stood up. "So, what's it gon' be? Am I your woman, or not?" She had her small fists clenched tight at her sides, her eyebrows furrowed.

I looked down on her and wanted to laugh. It's not that I wasn't taking her seriously, it was just that she was so fine and so little that I found that shit adorable. There was no way I could go without my li'l baby being in my life. I didn't think I was ready to be on some monogamous shit wit' her, but she didn't need to know that right then. I just had to say whatever it took to keep her centered in the moment. I would deal wit' the day-by-day after that.

I held her shoulders and looked into her pretty eyes. "It's

me and you, boo. I ain't finna let nothing or nobody come in between us. Period. I got a lot of work to do, but ain't no bitch about to steal your slot. I need to get my chips up so we can bounce from the east coast and live our lives together, along wit' Lonnie. You're my baby girl. Never forget that."

She shuddered and wrapped her arms around my waist. "Jahmani, I am very possessive when it comes to you. I will kill a bitch over you quick, and if you ever think you're going to up and leave me for anybody else, I swear to God above I will take you out the game. Don't take my kindness for weakness. I'm so far from what you think I am. Trust me when I tell you this." She took a step back. "My cousin Stephan rolls in tonight. He's a animal. If you're thinking we need to get our chips together, he's going to be the one I put you in tune with out here in North Carolina. That nigga is nuts, just like you. How much paper you think we need before we blow the east coast, anyway?"

"Depends on how good you trying to live. If we're thinking sensibly, at least five hundred thousand. That should last us a year, and by that time I should have run into a plethora of other licks. Sooner or later I'm going to have to find something legit and stable. We gotta think about our long-term futures, and Lonnie's."

Misty stepped away from me and turned her back. "Do you still have a thing for Ari? Huh, Jahmani? I need you to be real wit' me. If you do, I think I gotta handle my bidness wit' her. I still don't know how strong y'all relationship was before we came to be, but you crossed over to me pretty easily, so it couldn't have been that strong. However, her presence keeps nagging in the back of my mind. Something is telling me to get rid of her. Matter fact, where is she, anyway?"

I slid my arm around her neck. "She in a telly, out the way. Shawty ain't looking to cause no problems. You're overthinking everythang."

Misty shook her head. "It's impossible to overthink. And it could prove to be deadly if a person under-thinks things. Which hotel is she staying at? I wanna know right now."

"She at the Hilton, shawty. Why?"

She shook her head. "Oh, no reason for now. I just wanted to know. That's all." Misty slid her arms around my neck. "I ain't finna be okay about you, daddy. You are mine, and I'ma show you what a ride-or-die bitch really is. Mark my words on that." She kissed my cheek. "Now, come on. Let's get fresh before my cousin get here." She grabbed ahold of my wrist and pulled me toward the house.

I had a million thoughts going through my mind. It seemed as if Misty was growing up right before my eyes and becoming more like myself. I didn't know if I liked that or if I feared what she would transform into next. Either way, she was all I had in the moment, and my feelings for her were beginning to develop at a rampant pace.

Chapter 8

I was a lone wolf and never really got the hang of fuckin' wit' other niggas or rolling in packs. I was the type that liked to do damn near everything by myself and didn't take too kindly to other dudes, but I knew I was gon' jam wit' Stephan right away.

He arrived in town at eight o'clock later that night, and after Vicki introduced him as her son, we all sat down and had some of her infamous ghost pepper chili. Stephan was dark as night with brown eyes and a slim frame. He stood at about five feet, nine inches tall and had two red teardrops under his right eye. I could tell by the way he communicated with the woman he was from the slums of Baltimore.

Vicki couldn't take her eyes off him. She laughed at everything he said, and it seemed she couldn't help rubbing his cheek or hugging him between bites of his chili. I think the entire time she had a smile on her face while we ate our meal, and I gotta say the chili was fire. The best I'd had in my entire life, with its huge chunks of ground beef and sliced peppers that blended with the rest of the hidden flavors. She knew what she was doing in that kitchen, that was for sure.

After the meal, Stephan was about to head upstairs behind Vicki when Misty caught him. "Say, Stephan, can I talk to you right quick?" she asked, looking past him to a clearly annoyed Vicki.

"Misty, I ain't seen my son in damn near three months. I wanna spend some time wit' him. Now, can't you talk to him in the morning?" Vicki chastised.

"Oh, Aunty, this will only take a few minutes. I promise he'll be right back upstairs," Misty assured.

Stephan looked back at Misty. "Kid, what's this pertaining to? I kinda wanna chill wit' my moms." He looked up at Vicki and smiled. She blushed and looked off.

"Just give me a few minutes of your time, damn. You'll be back up there in no time."

Stephan glanced over to Vicki again. "Moms, g'on 'head and get the movie started. I'll be up there in a minute, a'ight?"

She nodded. "Okay, baby."

Stephan came down the steps and placed his arm around Misty's shoulders. "Shorty, you keep getting finer and finer, you know that."

She pushed his arm from around her. "Yeah, I know, but that's my animal right there." She nodded her head to me.

I stood up from the couch with Lonnie in my arms. She was knocked out. I laid her out on the sofa and kissed her cheek. "Yo, let's holler in the den."

They led the way. When we got there, Misty waited until I stepped inside of the room before she lightly closed the door behind me. I took a seat on the couch, and so did Stephan.

"Yo, Stephan, nigga, I already know the only time you be touching down in Greenville is when you got some shit up your sleeve. I don't know what it is or what the job entails, but I want you to let my nigga trap wit' you. He a savage from the Bronx. That nigga 'bout that life, just like you are. If not more," she added.

Stephan laughed and looked to me. "Say, money, you put ya earth up to dis shit?"

"Nall, son, she was just telling me you 'bout that scratch. I'm in a time crunch. I need some quick paper, and I need it, like, ASAP. I don't give a fuck what I gotta do to get it. Also, I'm pretty sure you know somebody that's looking for some good-good." I grabbed the Batman book bag, unzipped it, and took out six of the bricks I'd gotten from the Doughboy and PT lick. "Pure tar, baby, right here. Over seventy percent."

Stephan picked up one of the bricks and sat it on the table.

He pulled out a Swiss Army knife. "May I?"

I nodded.

He poked it and came up within a significant amount. He put the blade to his nose and sniffed, jerked his head back, and coughed. He closed his eyes tight, shaking his head from side to side. "Damn, damn, damn. That shit hitting. I feel it. Yo, this shit sauce, kid. We can use these to open a few doors. Yo, but how do I know that you get down? Just 'cause you from New York don't make you a hitta. I know plenty fuck-niggas from out there."

"I don't give a fuck who you knew, I'm Jahmani Mayweather. It ain't no nigga out there like me. I stand in my own lane. You wanna know what it is, then just test me."

Stephan pulled his nose. He cleared the knife with his right nostril, coughed, and squeezed his eyes tight. "Yeah, a'ight, I'ma fuck wit' you first thang in the morning. We gon' see where your heart at. You perform the right way and I'll get you right real fast. You can bank on that."

Misty shook her head. "Cuz, you don't need to treat him like he one of these North Carolina wimps or something. My man come certified."

Stephan pulled his nose again and laughed. "Yo, kid, you always let your woman do all the talking for you?" He wiped the knife on his pant leg and put it away.

I fixed the puncture in the package, then put my bricks back in the bag. "I'll correct her and tell her to shut her ass up when I disagreed with something she saying. So far she's verbally representing me quite well. I ain't no country bumpkin, that's all I'ma say."

Stephan staggered a bit on his feet. He pointed at the book bag. "Nall, that shit right there ain't playing. But, like I said, kid, we gon' fuck around in the morning. I'ma see what it do then. For now, the rest of this night belongs to my moms.

Peace, y'all."

I watched him slowly find his way out of the room. Misty walked up to me and kissed my lips. "Daddy, that nigga be hitting all types of licks. He don't even come to visit unless he got some shit up his sleeve that's worth some major chips. You gotta stay close to him until we figure something else out. While I'm here, I'ma make a few phone calls to see what's good. If our target number is five hundred thousand, then I got some work to do." She wrapped her arms around my neck and laid her cheek on my chest.

I liked hearing her talk about making moves. That both excited and turned me on. She had me looking at her in a different light. I held her tighter, then leaned my head down and tongued her ass down, gripping that fat ass the entire time. "Shawty, why it sound like you turning into me?"

"'Cause I'm my daddy's rib. How can you expect me to not turn into you when I come from you? That don't make any sense." She rolled her eyes.

I licked her neck. "Oh, you come from me, huh. You my baby?" My hands pulled up her skirt and slipped into her thong from the back. Her lips were already exposed. My fingers played over them.

"Yes," she breathed. "You know I am, daddy. Look at me. I even got light freckles on my face like you."

I picked her ass up. She wrapped her thick thighs around me. I held her cheeks in my palms. We continued to tongue each other down, breathing hard and heavy. I sat her on the den's table, laid her back, and opened her thighs. The crotch band of the thong went directly up the center of her cleft. There was a pussy lip poking out on each side of it. "You're my baby, right?"

She opened her thighs wider. "Yes, daddy. I'm your rib. I'm your baby." She pulled her crotch band to the side and opened her pussy lips wide, exposing her bubblegum-colored insides. "Taste me, daddy. I need you to. Please." Her middle finger trailed circles around her bud.

I sucked up her left thigh and rubbed her pussy with my right hand. She was on fire. After coating them with her juices, I sucked each finger into my mouth one at a time. Then my face was between her thighs. My tongue invaded her slit, licking in between the folds before twirling around her clitoris. Her scent was nice and strong with a hint of perfume. I got to nibbling on her vagina's nipple.

She shuddered. "Ooh. Ooh. Daddy. Yes. Ooh. Un." She threw her head back and held her lips wide open for me.

I licked all over her fingers, pussy, and everything. Her juices were leaking out of her. I couldn't help slurping it up like soup. When I started to finger her, she got to going crazy on the table.

"Cum for daddy, baby. Cum for me."

Her thighs opened wider. Her nipples were spiked through her shirt. She pinched them and screamed, then came all into my mouth while I swallowed and slurped some more.

I wound up on my back with Misty on top of me, riding away. She held my chest and fucked like a horny porn star. I pulled her shirt over her head because I wanted to see them pretty titties bounce while she did her thing. I liked the way her nipples looked, all distended and shit. They were dark brown and covered a nice portion of her breasts. I held her ass while she rode me faster and faster, my fingers digging into the meat of it.

"Daddy. Uh, daddy. I'm cumming, daddy. Aw, fuck, I love you. I love you. Un, shit!" She sucked my neck and came all over my pipe, rolling her hips hard.

I flipped her over and forced her knees to her chest. That opened that pussy all the way up. I knelt there for a minute, just watching how her cream oozed out of her. It sailed from her pussy into her ass crack, wetting a path along the way. I licked it up and sucked loudly on her cleft again before sliding into her and banging home hard. Her cushion felt amazing. I got to trying to beat her box out of the frame.

Bam. Bam. Bam. Bam.

She dug her nails into my back, and dragged them downward. "Uh, fuck! Shit, baby!"

Harder and harder. This was my pussy. My baby. My rib. Every time I got between these thighs, it was a must that I gave her ass the bidness. Plus, she had a wet shot that encouraged me to go hard. It felt so good. Not only was I feeling some type of way about her, but she had me falling in love with her pussy, too. I got to fucking her so hard it was like I was trying to nail her to the floor. Her face went through a series of contortions. She was breathing just as hard as I was. Her pussy walls sucked at me. I continued to drill, feeling her nails dig into my back.

"I'm finna cum in this pussy, baby. Daddy finna cum. Aw, shit, baby. Mm." I sped up the pace and pressed her knees even harder into her breasts, then I was cumming hard over and over, jerking like crazy.

She allowed me to finish before she twisted from under me and took ahold of my piece. She sucked her juices off it, squeezed me hard in her fist, and pulled it all the way to the top of my head, milking me. A dab of semen appeared on the top of my helmet. She licked it off, then sucked on my top, drinking my seed. I shivered and dug my nails into the carpet until she finished me off.

***

After we finished fucking, I got hungry. We tiptoed into

the kitchen and got to making cold cut sandwiches, laughing and smelling like sex. It was crazy for me, trying to navigate through Vicki's kitchen in the dark. Me and Misty kept bumping into each other. That would cause me to snatch her ass up and suck all over her neck. Then she was gripping my dick again. Before I knew it, she was bent over holding the counter, and I was fuckin' her hard from the back while I used the refrigerator light to watch my dick shoot in and out of her. I even opened her ass cheeks so I could see her li'l crinkle.

After cumming twice in the kitchen, we grabbed our food and made our way up the stairs. When I was halfway up them, I heard the distinct music of Gerald Levert. The air smelled funny. Then there was the constant tapping of a headboard against a wall and bedsprings going haywire. I frowned and looked down at Misty. "Yo, you hear that shit?" I whispered.

She stopped and perked up, I guessed to see if she could hear what I did. "What?"

"The bedsprings. You smell the air? It smell like sex."

She sniffed harder, then shrugged her shoulders. "I don't smell nothing. I think you're smelling us. Come on, let's get in our room before we stank up the hallway." She rushed off ahead of me and into the room we were staying in.

I stepped into the hallway holding my food. When I came to Vicki's door, I got nosey and placed my ear upon it. The bedsprings appeared louder. So did the tapping and Gerald Levert. I could also hear moaning. I didn't give a fuck what Misty was talking about, somebody was definitely in there screwing. All of the signs were there.

"Psst. Come on, Jahmani, damn. Stop being all nosey and shit," she whispered, waving for me to hurry up.

I sniffed the air one last time, then stepped into our room. She closed the door behind me.

"Dang, I ain't never saw you be so nosey before. You

listening all at my aunt's door and shit. That ain't cool." She set her food on the night table and took mine out of my hands.

I was still curious. "Shawty, tell me something? Now, I don't wanna sound too off base here or disrespect yo' people, but is they in there fucking?"

Misty lowered her head and waved me off. "Jahmani, don't go there. Whatever they in there doing, it ain't got nothing to do wit' you and I. We in here. That's all I got to say."

Now my eyes were open like windows on a spring day. "What? Hell nall! Now I wanna know. They in there fucking? Fo' real?" I was confused.

"Nall. Nall. I didn't' say that. You're saying that. I'm saying whatever they are in there doing, it ain't our business." She blushed and turned brighter than I'd ever seen her.

I opened the door and looked down the hallway. "Damn, y'all family crazy as hell. I knew Vicki li'l fine ass had something going on behind them brown eyes of hers. Shawty look like she 'bout that taboo shit. Damn." I shook my head. I was intrigued and wondered how all that shit kicked off.

Misty made her way across the room and stood in front of me. "Oh, so you think she fine, huh?" She curled her top lip and balled my wife beater into her fist.

I laughed and closed the door, moving her back. "Shawty, yo' aunty bad. I can see y'all got some good genes, though. That don't mean you gotta get all jealous and shit. You still the baddest bitch in this house."

"Mm-hm, I better be. You better stop peeping my aunty, too. Ain't shit moving. Nigga, you belong to me. I done already told yo' ass. Word-up." She grabbed me by my dick and pulled me toward the food. "Jahmani, when you go wit' that nigga tomorrow, don't be asking him about him and Vicki's relationship. Just rock wit' him so you can get that paper. Don't shit else concern us, and keep in mind that this is the South. You gon' see a whole lot of stuff that's gon' leave you scratching your head. Just roll wit' it."

I sat my plate on my lap and bit into my sandwich. I didn't care what took place in North Carolina as long as I was going to be able to get my money up. "Shawty, you good. You ain't gotta worry about me picking at your family secrets," I laughed. "I still find that shit intriguing, though." I kissed her cheek and tore into my food. I definitely wanted to get to know Vicki better. I still couldn't believe her li'l thick ass was getting down like that.

Ghost

Chapter 9

"A'ight, Jahmani, we about to go in here and holler at this fool named Rambo. He a old head that been moving weight through the city for about fifteen years. He got his hands in a little bit of everything, and when it comes to busting moves, this nigga know what's really good. Him and my pops used to roll together back in the day before my old man got killed in Philly. I'ma tell him you my cousin, and we gon' go from there." He finished his Maverick cigarette and flicked it out of the window. We were sitting inside his Lincoln Navigator. He had all-black leather seats with his name stitched into the headrests. It felt cozy.

"Why the fuck we finna go and see this nigga again?" I asked, pulling my nine from under the seat and placing it in the small of my back.

"Because bruh gon' line us up with a few licks and pay us real good for them. You see, he one of them real shysty niggas. He's the type that'll supply you with a nice amount of work, but then send a nigga like me to come and get that shit back from you. He a shark, and I'm telling you the only reason why I'm fuckin' wit' this cat is because he was plugged wit' my pops. He gon' tell us what's good, we gon' hit a few niggas, and we should have at least a few hunnit thousand apiece before the end of the week. That sound good to you, kid?"

"Hell yeah. Long as everything you saying is authentic, I'm all in. Let's roll." I pulled my shirt over my waist and grabbed the handle to the truck, ready to get out.

Stephan grabbed my shoulder. "Yo, hold up, kid. You ain't about to be able to step into that nigga setup with no pistol on you. Them muthafuckas finna pat us down at the door, believe that." He reached under the seat and came up with an Uzi. "If it was sweet, I'd be bringing this muthafucka in there wit' me."

I frowned. "Yo, I don't know this nigga. You saying he be on all type of shysty shit. Why the fuck wouldn't we go through that bitch wit' these bangers on us? This fool finna make some sort of an exception or something."

Stephan shook his head. "It don't work like that, B. We gotta roll without our swords. It is what it is. Welcome to Greenville." He opened his truck door. "Leave that muthafucka under the seat and let's ride out."

I reluctantly followed his commands. I felt naked as hell doing such, but as far as I was concerned, I was a long way from the dramas of the Bronx and New York as a whole. I prayed I wouldn't run into any enemies, and if I did, I'd have to improvise.

I jumped out of his whip and followed close behind him. We strolled down a short dirt road that led into a vacant field. The sun beaming like crazy. There wasn't a breeze in sight, and it had to be every bit of ninety-plus degrees outside and humid. By the time we made it through the field and up to the two-story white house, I was hot and sticky. My shirt was sticking to me. Even though I was goin' into a foreign territory, I was kinda glad I hadn't put on my bulletproof vest. I would've really been sweating.

We stepped to the side door of the crib, and Stephan knocked three times and took a step back. His eyes were directed upward, so I decided to look up as well.

About thirty seconds after he'd knocked on the door, a dark-skinned man with long dreadlocks and glasses stuck an AK-47 out of the window and peered through the scope. "Who the fuck is dat beating on my muthafuckin' do', mane?"

Stephan threw up his arms. "Nigga, put that shit away. It's Stephan son. Open the do', god."

"Yeah, I see you, but who is that other nigga that's wit' you?"

Now he had the Kay aimed at me. I fidgeted and eased out of his line of fire. I was wishing I'da worn my vest now and brought my pistol. If I had my nine on me, I would have busted through that window and wet his ass up. "Yo, son, tell ya mans to ease off of his trigger, kid," I advised Stephan.

"Yo, Rambo, chill the fuck out. This my cousin Jahmani from New York. Son one hunnit, just like me. You know I ain't finna bring no peons around here, pa. Ring that muthafucka in. It's good."

The dark-skinned man mugged him for a few more seconds, and then he pulled the Kay into the window and shut it. We waited for two minutes, and then he opened the door with a big blunt in his mouth. He smiled as thick clouds of smoke poured out of his nose. "Get against the house and assume the position. Stephan, you already know what it is."

Stephan tapped my shoulder. "Come on, bruh. He just wanna make sure we ain't got shit on us. That's all."

I didn't, so I assumed the position. I placed my hands on the house directly next to Stephan's. The gangway was narrow. I looked from side to side and already felt violated before anybody laid hands on me.

A light-skinned chick came from the side door and patted us down, first Stephan, and then me. After confirming we were clean, she took a step back into the house and stood behind Rambo.

Rambo looked me up and down. "You say his name Jahmani, huh?"

"Yeah. He my cousin, and he gon' help me take this shit to the next level. Before you write him off, all you gotta do is put us up on something."

Rambo placed his finger to his lips. "Shh. Y'all come on in." He looked both ways, opened the door, and stepped to the side.

Stephan entered first, and I was a few steps behind him. When I got inside, it smelled like heavy loud. It was so strong I caught a high right away. He led us up the stairs and into his crib. Once inside, he instructed us to take seats on the couch. Directly in front of us was a punch bowl full of yellow weed. "Help yourselves."

Stephan took a Dutch wrap from beside the punch bowl and began to roll him a blunt. He made sure he took big chunks, spaced them out accordingly, and rolling up.

I was unfamiliar with this Rambo nigga. I wasn't trying to be high. I was trying to remain as lucid as the secondhand smoke would allow me to so I could peep this new nigga and read him as best I could. When it came to surviving in the game, reading and dissecting those around me was the first key to survival. I knew that, which is why I carried on like I did.

"Yo, son, you ain't rolling up?" Stephan asked, sparking his L.

"Nall, kid, I'm good. What's the bidness, though?" I wanted to get things moving along. I didn't like being in places where I was unarmed and at the mercy of another nigga. I wanted to get out if there as fast as I could.

"A'ight," Stephan nodded at Rambo. "Yo, what's the move, son. What you got for us?"

Rambo smacked the redbone who had searched both Stephan and myself on the ass. "Shawty, g'on in the other room and finish counting that money. I'll be in there in a minute. Let me get some shit together. I'll be in there to help in a minute." He sat the AK-47 on the table in front of him.

She kissed his cheek and walked away with her ass jiggling in the jogging pants. I kept my eyes on her all the way until she left the room. I found her alluring because she was just a bit bowlegged. She still ain't have shit on Misty, though.

"You see something you like, boy?" Rambo growled.

I scoffed. "Not really. I just ain't never seen no bowlegged chick before, that's it."

"Well, that bowlegged chick is my daughter, and I don't play about her. Now, y'all come over here to do bidness, let's stick to that," he mugged me.

I wanted to check this chump in the raw. I didn't know who the fuck he thought he was, but had this been New York, I would have laid him down along with his mediocre-ass daughter, especially since he gave her the command to go into the other room and count some money.

"Yo, it's good, Rambo. The homey from out of town. He peeped Lea, and that's it. No disrespect intended. Now, what you got for me?"

Rambo blew smoke toward me and continued to mug me. "Yeah, that's all it better be. That's my li'l girl right there. I'll kill a nigga over her quick."

I clenched my jaw off and on. I was seconds away from popping off at his ass. "Man, you safe. I wasn't even jocking her on that level, trust me. She ain't my type. I fuck wit' pure dimes. Always have."

Rambo sat his blunt on the ashtray and looked over to me. "What's that supposed to mean?"

My temper was beginning to boil. "Exactly what the fuck I said. You safe. Even if she wasn't spoken for, she wouldn't have to worry about me speaking to her. I like bad bitches."

Rambo jumped up. "You betta watch yo' mouth, li'l nigga. You skating a thin line right now."

Now I was up on my feet. "Nigga, I ain't better watch shit. Matter fact," I grabbed the AK-47 from the table and cocked that bitch. "Pussy-nigga, the Bronx in the building. Lay it the fuck down. Now!"

"Jahmani, what the fuck you doing, man?" Stephan hollered, standing up.

I slapped Rambo with my left hand and pressed the Kay to his ribs. "Fuck this nigga, kid. Son acting like he need some respect, so I'ma give his bitch-ass some. Go in there and get that money from that ugly-ass bitch."

"You making a grave mistake, li'l nigga. You don't know who you're dealing wit'," Rambo warned with a trace of blood running down the side of his mouth.

"Oh, you think so? Well, fuck it, then." I aimed at his knees.

Boom. Boom. Boom.

The bullets shred through his knees and knocked them out of his extremities. He fell to the ground, hollering in pain.

"Fuck!" Stephan took off running toward the back of the house. He busted in the room door, then I could hear a scream and a bunch of tussling.

I kicked Rambo in the ribs. "How much money you got in this house, homie? Huh? You got enough to save you and your daughter's life?"

He fell onto his back and tried to get back up. He used the couch and climbed up on it. He held his hands in the air as the tussling continued to take place in the other room. "Look, man, it's a hundred thousand here. My daughter counting it on the bed in the other room. Y'all can take every penny. Just leave us with our lives, Jahmani. What do you say, huh?"

Stephan came into the room holding Lea around the neck with a knife to it. "If we leave this nigga alive, he gon' definitely come after us. We started this shit, now we gotta finish it." He sliced her throat and tossed her to the floor. "Smoke that fool."

I aimed at Rambo and pulled the trigger. He curled into a ball as the rounds ate away at him, knocking big holes into his body. He seemed to vibrate before fading away into a puddle of his own blood.

Stephan shook his head. "Yeah, I can already see we finna have some fun. Come on, let's bag this money and get the fuck out of here.

***

Twenty minutes later we were settling into the den with a table full of money. I separated what looked like half, and started to count the spoils while Stephan sat across the table and did the same thing.

"Yo, I gotta give you yo' props, Bronx kid, you handled that bidness wit' no regard. I could tell he had you feeling some type of way, how you kept on mugging him and shit. That bitch got him twisted. He'll be a'ight, though," he laughed and started to count his stacks.

I was counting away. "Son, there was no way I was going to be able to take orders from a nigga like him. Kid was way too cocky for his own good. Besides, I ain't no send-off. If we gon' run through this bitch, it's gon' be by our own accord, not by some goofy-ass nigga trying to call shots over us. Fuck that."

Stephan laughed. "Fuck it, then, we just gon' wreck the whole city and turn this bitch upside down. I know a few spots we can hit to get our chips up. You still funny to me, though. Bruh said 'fuck that.' He stood over that nigga and dumped about fifteen slugs in his ass. Now, that's my type of nigga. I guess my cousin wasn't jacking on yo' name. You definitely 'bout that life."

I didn't like this nigga being all on my dick like a bitch. His words were only irritating me. I was never seeking his approval; I just did what I wanted to do in the moment. Wasn't nobody finna treat me like a ho-nigga and think it was sweet. "Bruh, that shit over wit'. Let's get on something new."

There was a knock at the door. Stephan perked up. "Yo, who is it?"

"It's Misty. Where my daddy at?" she asked in a whiney voice.

"Yo, he doing something. Go sit yo' ass down somewhere," he ordered.

I felt offended right away. I jumped up and a bundle of cash fell off my lap. I opened the door and Misty stepped into my arms. I wrapped them around her. "Aye, say, Stephan, don't talk to my shawty like that in front of me. This my rib, right here. Ain't shit finna go on between us that she don't know about."

"Damn, that's my bad, god. It's good," he joked.

Misty mugged him and looked around at all of the money. "I take it y'all handled a li'l bidness, daddy?"

I nodded. "Yeah, and we just getting started."

Chapter 10

A week after Stephan strolled into town, Ari hit me up and said she wanted me to come and get her. She said she had a surprise for me that was sure to blow my socks off. I didn't know about all that, but after me and Stephan hit another lick that grossed ten gees apiece, I had him stroll by the Hilton. He pulled up at five in the evening and threw his truck in park.

"Yo, son, how long you finna be up there? I'm drowsy as a muthafucka. I been up for two days straight fuckin' wit' my moms on some late-night kicking-it shit." He yawned and covered his mouth with his right hand.

I glanced up at the building. "Probably for about an hour. You're more than welcome to come up if you want to."

He waved me off. "Nall, I'm finna chill and close my eyes for that li'l hour. Just hit my phone before you come back down. I'm finna turn up this J. Cole."

"That's what's up. I'ma fuck wit' you in a minute." I closed his door and jogged across the parking lot. It was just starting to drizzle outside. I was low-key thankful for the rain. Ever since I'd been down in North Carolina it had been hot and humid.

I made it inside and up to Ari's room in about ten minutes. I knocked on the door. A few moments passed before she pulled it open with a smile on her pretty caramel face. Her lips were shined up with gloss. "What's good, Jahmani? You miss me?"

I sucked my teeth, brushed past her, and tried my best to not focus on how fine she looked. She even smelled good, too. That was one of my weaknesses when it came to a woman. "Yo, what's the emergency, goddess?"

She closed the door and looked me over. "I never said there was any emergency. I said I have something for you that is going to knock your socks off." She loosened the sash around her robe and held it open to reveal the two-piece, pink-and-black, matching Victoria's Secret set. The material was see-through. I could make out her pussy lips and the big, dark areolas of her nipples. "How do you know I wasn't talking about all of this?"

My eyes damn near bugged out of my head. "Damn, shawty, you betta close that robe before you get in trouble."

She smiled and tied the sash back, stepped across the room, and stood in front of me. "I been missing you, Jahmani. You act like I don't even exist no more. I can barely get a goodnight text out of you at night." She placed her right hand on the side of my face. I could smell her moisturizer.

My hands held her slim waist. I trailed them around and cupped that ass. I couldn't help it. It was like when it came to bad women, my body acted on autopilot. Ari was fine as a muthafucka, too, and I also had an emotional connection to her because we had been through so much. Visions of Misty continued to nag at me, so I dropped my hands and backed away. "Ari, what's good wit' you?"

She stepped forward again. Now her nose was against mine. "Ain't nothin' good wit' me. I been missing you like crazy, and that's all there is to it. I want my man back. I should've never lost you, especially not to her." She swiped at my lips with her tongue, then sucked the bottom one into her mouth. "Mm, Jahmani, it's been so long. When am I gon' get some of my baby daddy?"

I kissed her for a minute and stepped back, wiping my lips with the back of my hand. "Ari, you bugging. You know you ain't fuckin' wit' me on that level. You're up to something. I don't know what it is, but I ain't got time for it." I dug in my pocket and pulled out five gees. "Huh, this a li'l pocket change for you."

She grabbed it out of my hand and threw it on the bed, wrapped her arms around my neck, and sucked all over my lips. Then she trailed down to my neck and sucked hard on it. I could feel her teeth biting and sucking. "Un. I want you, Jahmani. I'm fien'ing right now. I don't give a fuck if you go back to her. I want you right now." She squeezed my piece and unbuckled my belt, sank to her knees, and pulled my dick out, stroking it. "I want some of my baby daddy."

My back hit the wall. I felt her tongue lick the helmet, and then she sucked it into her mouth. It felt good, I can't lie, but I couldn't get Misty off of my brain. I knew she would go bananas if she found out I was fuckin' Ari again. I didn't want to hurt her like that. Against all odds, she was still my baby.

I slid to my right and broke Ari's hold on my dick. My piece popped out of her mouth with a loud suction noise. "Yo, I can't fuck wit' you like this, Ari. I ain't on that no more."

She licked her lips and stood up. "You ain't on what no more?"

I fixed my pants. "Yo, we ain't gotta get into it. You already know what I'm talking about, though."

She winced and bucked her eyes. "Aw, so now you one of those faithful niggas? You cheat on me with my cousin, then what? You call yourself wife-ing her and shitting on me after I get pregnant with your kid? What type of shit is that?" She bumped me and flared her nostrils.

I blew air through my teeth to calm myself down. I tossed her to the bed. "Get yo' li'l ass out my face. I said what I said. I'm trying to turn over a new leaf. Do right by shawty." I said that last part just to get on her nerves a li'l bit.

She bounced off the bed and balled her fists. "Jahmani, I swear to God if I wasn't pregnant, I would do my best to stomp a mud hole in your ass. Don't you ever say that shit to me again!" She pointed her finger in my face.

I bit that muthafucka and pushed her out of my face. When she landed on the bed, I sat beside her and placed my hand on her stomach. "How my li'l one doing?"

She brushed by hand away. "Get the fuck off me and don't worry about it." She tried to get up.

I pulled her back down. "Stop playin' wit' me. What have you been eating?"

"Jahmani, I swear to God, you better get off me. You got some fuckin' nerve asking me how our child is doing when all you've done is leave me in this hotel alone ever since we've touched down in North Carolina. You don't care how this baby is doing, nor myself. But that's okay, because I don't need your ass, either." She broke away from me and pulled on a pair of pants. "You know what? I'm taking my ass back to New York. I don't know what I'ma do when I get there yet, but whatever I do is gon' be better than what you're taking me through down here. This shit hurts." She blinked back tears and continued to get dressed.

I stood a short distance away, in the middle of the room with by head down. "Ari, you can't go back to New York. We're wanted up there. They gon' put yo' ass up under the jail. Is that what you want?"

She smacked her lips. "I don't even care no more, Jahmani. I ain't got shit to live for out here. My brother was all I had left, and you took him away from me. I still can't understand how you can continuously shit on me, knowing you killed my people, and you make it seem like it ain't no big deal. You choosing my cousin over me, even though I saved this nigga's life and carrying his baby. If that ain't trifling, then please tell me what is." She took a suitcase out of the closet and began to pack a few items of clothes I guessed she'd purchased during our time down there.

"Ari, I'm sorry. I was just fucking wit' you shawty, damn.

Come here."

She ignored me and continued to pack. "Nall, it's good Jahmani. I know where we stand now. You ain't rocking wit' me no more. I can get that through my big head. It ain't that hard." She walked past me, "Excuse me," bent over, and picked up a pair of Air Max. She put them inside the suitcase. "I just wanna let you know the slug I took in my side for you still hurts. The fact I took Doughboy's life for you still haunts me at night. I see his face in my dreams asking me why. I still see my brother's, too. I loved you, Jahmani. I still do, but it's clear it's one-sided. All you care about is yourself. I finally get it." She slammed the bag on the bed and lowered her face into her hands.

Damn, I felt like shit. I truly didn't understand how many losses I'd handed to her until she spelled them out like that. I had been bogus to her. I had to be better. She was carrying my child, and she was the reason both myself and Lonnie had life inside our bodies. I sat beside her on the bed. "Ari, I'm sorry. I know I been real distant and bogus toward you, but I'ma be better. I owe you more than what I been giving you. I swear I'm sorry."

"It's whatever, Jahmani. I mean, the writing is on the wall. You don't care about me, and all I want to know is why? Why don't you give a damn about me? And what has she done that has allowed you to fall in love with her so quickly? Please tell me that." She wiped tears from her eyes.

I hung my head, speechless. "That shit don't matter right now, Ari. I need to know what I can do to make you feel better. What can I do to heal you?"

Ari hopped up, tears dripping from her chin. "You can't just make something right in a split second, Jahmani. I've taken a lot of losses ever since I've been involved with you. I've only seen the best version of you for about a month. Other than that, you've treated me like crap. Then, to know you love the woman you cheated on me with so much that I can't even lay down with you shatters my soul. I mean, what does she have that I don't?"

"Shawty, it ain't about what she got over you. It's about how we are together. Misty is like my li'l baby. She real clingy and affectionate. We don't be arguing about every little thing like you and I do. In addition to that, when I jam wit' shawty, it's like I can tell she really for me. That in the end she gon' be standing by my side. I don't know if I really see that shit wit' you. Wit' us it's like we're cool today, but will we be snaking each other tomorrow?"

She turned her back to me and shook her head. I could hear a sob escape her throat. "Do you have any idea how much pain you've put me through? And I'm still right here standing by yo' trifling-ass side. Jahmani, you killed my brother. You took my brother's life, and I could've set you up to be killed, but instead I helped you escape with your life. And you think Misty has proven herself to you more than I have? Are you fuckin' serious? Are you?" She took a deep breath and turned around to face me. "I don't know what else I can do, Jahmani. All you gotta do is tell me. Tell me what you want from me. I'm breaking into pieces here." She wiped snot away from her nose and stepped closer. "I'm weak. I don't have nobody. Nobody. I'm in this world all alone."

The way her voice was breaking up was getting the better of me. I hated to see those I was familiar with in any type of pain. I pulled her into my arms. "Ari, I got you. Stop saying that 'you're all alone' shit. That's not the case. I got you, baby. I'll never let you fend for yourself."

She wrapped her arms around my waist. "I remember how you pursued me, Jahmani. You made me feel so good. You kept coming and coming. No matter the dangers you faced, you kept on trying. We've saved each other's lives. But now I'm drowning again. I need you to save me so I can be strong enough to save you in the future. I need you so badly." She tilted her head backward and kissed my lips.

Even though I wanted to pull back, I couldn't. Her energy was weighing heavy on the few emotions I possessed for her, or anybody for that matter. In the short amount of time we'd been a part of one another, we'd been forced to fight through the pain of so many losses. There was only one way for us to heal one another.

Ghost

Chapter 11

I sucked on her bottom lip, then the top one. I gripped her ass in the form-fitting Gucci jeans, unbuttoned them, drug them down her thighs, and left them there. My hand traveled between her thighs. I rubbed her juicy box. The lips were plump and engorged. I went into the waistband and cupped that monkey.

"Aw, Jahmani." Her thighs opened as far as the jeans around her thighs would allow. She yanked her panties down, and they stopped mid-thigh as well. "I want some so bad, Jahmani. My kitty is meowing in there. Can I suck you to get you ready? Please?"

My dick was already rock-hard. I stepped back and pulled my jeans down and off, then stood there stroking him. "Come on, baby. Get you some."

She took ahold of it and knelt back to the carpet. "I just want you to love me, Jahmani. Can you love me more than you love her? It was us before y'all." She sucked me into her mouth and speared her face over and over again, then popped me out. "Answer me, baby." She got to sucking me at a rapid pace.

My eyes rolled back. My toes curled. I tried to block out images of Misty. Every time I saw her face in my mind's eye, I started to go soft. I didn't know what was wrong wit' me. Nothing like that had ever happened before.

Ari took her mouth away and stroked him faster, looking up at me. She squeezed me in her fist. "Do you still want me, Jahmani? Huh? Just be honest?"

I had my eyes closed, trying to think of anything other than the fact I couldn't get Misty out of my mind. I felt like I was betraying her in a major way. "Yeah, baby, I want you. I been wanting you ever since I met you. Handle yo' bidness." I put by fingers into her hair and tangled them, led her mouth back to my pipe, and inserted him. He was only at about half-mast. That was aggravating.

Ari licked along my length and sucked me back into her mouth again. She went to work for a full two minutes and popped me out. "Damn, Jahmani!" She stood up and sat on the bed, lowering her face to her hands again.

I pulled my pants back on, along wit' my boxers. "Yo, I must be tired or some shit. That ain't never happened to me before. But I have been up trapping for the last two days. Maybe we should try this again later or something?"

"Yo' penis got a conscience, Jahmani."

"What?"

She removed her hands from her face. "You heard what I said. Your penis has a conscience. You've actually fallen in love with Misty. It's gotten to the point that when I'm doing what I'm supposed to down there, it's not staying hard. It's either that or you no longer desire me. Either way, it sucks for me all across the board." She started to get dressed. "I'm definitely getting the fuck out of here now. I don't know how much more I can take from you. You're mentally killing me more than any other situation we're faced with."

"Ari, I'm just tired. This shit ain't got nothing to do with anything else," I lied. Even as I stood there arguing with her or trying to convince her otherwise, I couldn't get Misty off my brain. I missed my baby girl like crazy. I couldn't wait to wrap her li'l ass up in my arms. I also missed the scent of her. I felt like I was turning pussy. I had to shake those feelings off quick. "Yo, come here for a second, shawty."

"Fuck you, Jahmani. I'm out of here. I'm tired of being at your mercy. I'm tired of feeling vulnerable. I'm tired of being rejected and made to feel second place. There is no woman on God's green earth that wants to be second to anybody. I am Eve. I was created to be first and most important at all times. I can't sit back and act like the relationship you have with my cousin isn't killing me right now, because it is. You cheated on me with her and wound up kicking me all the way to the curb for her after you impregnated me by damn near taking the pussy." She scoffed. "Now you got me in this mad jam, and I don't know what to do. I'm sitting around here, emotions all over the place and in need of any type of affection. So I call myself ready to put out just so I can get something emotionally from you, and you can't even perform, so I can't even get that. It's like, damn. Now I feel twice as rejected and three times more stupid. You are killing me." She slid her shirt back over her head.

Now I felt like a pure asshole. "Ari. Damn. Ma, I'm sorry. I'm telling you it ain't got nothing to do wit' none of that shit you saying right now. I just got a lot on my brain. Sex ain't at the top of the totem pole for a nigga. Com'ere." I pulled her to me.

She yanked away from my grasp. "Get off of me. I don't wanna hear that sympathetic shit, Jahmani. I bet you any money you ain't been having no problem fuckin' her, have you?"

"We ain't been fuckin' either," I lied. Even as I told her this, I imagined Misty's bald pussy and how it looked when I opened it and ran my tongue around her erect clitoris. My piece started to harden, and I knew I had a problem. "I'm telling you, Shawty, it's all this shit I'm up against. I got twelve on my ass for all the shit I did back in New York. On top of that, I gotta find a way to raise Lonnie and be there for her while I'm on the run. At the same time, I remain worried because any day I could wake up and the Feds could be standing over me. Then Linx still in the wind. I gotta get that fool Beans back for what he did to my people, and I gotta find Samantha. While all of this shit is flowing, I gotta get my chips up in the here and now so all of us can shake this side of the United States, because it's only a matter if time before we are popped off. That's a whole lot of thinking for one man to do. So, don't make this about you, because while you share a portion of my thoughts, it's not your shortcomings that have me unable to perform." I acted irritated, and I couldn't believe I could come up with such a spill spur-of-the-whim like that. While ninety percent of it was true, I didn't have no problem fucking Misty or feeling some type of way about Vicki. I think I was having trouble strictly because I felt like I was cheating on Misty with her enemy. Even though I was a grimy nigga, when it came to Misty, I couldn't betray her like that. The feelings were new for me.

My cellphone rang with a text from Stephan. "*Nigga, whut up? It's been ninety minutes.*"

I texted back, "*Ten minutes, and I'll be down.*"

Ari tried to rubberneck to see who I was texting. "That's her, ain't it?"

I shook my head. "Nall, that's one of my homeboys asking me when I'm finna come down." I turned the phone around so she could see his text and my response to it.

She frowned. "Hit him back and tell him he can pull off. That you chilling wit' me for the night." She placed her hand on her hip and gave me a stern look.

I laughed her off. "Shawty, you know damn well I can't do that. I ain't finna be arguing wit' Misty ass all night, plus I gotta take care of Lonnie. It's my night to tuck her in and read her a story."

"What the fuck? So, y'all playing house now? Kid, you over there acting like you got a family wit' her when you really are about to have one wit' me?"

She clenched her teeth and hauled off and slapped me. That shit rocked me, too, 'cause it caught me off guard. I stumbled backward into the dresser, holding my face. I closed my eyes because I felt myself steaming up.

"How the fuck you gon' do me like that, Jahmani? If anybody should be next to you while you're taking care of Lonnie, it should be me. I'm the one that helped you save her life. I saved yours, too. But you got me in some seedy-ass hotel while you lay-up in a house with Misty and that li'l girl. Nigga, I could kill yo' ass right now." She ran at me, swinging her fists in a windmill fashion. "I'ma kill you. I'ma kill you. I'ma kill you," she repeated over and over again while she rained down blows upon me.

I allowed about ten of them to connect before I side-stepped her ass and snatched her up, bear-hugging her. "Shawty, calm yo' ass down. What the fuck is wrong wit' you?" I snapped, feeling blood drip from my lip.

"Let me go, Jahmani. I'm finna kill yo' ass. I'm tired of this pain you're giving me. I can't take it no more. Let me go!"

She fought as hard as she could to get out of my grasp. The more she fought, the tighter I held her ass. I was so angry that I felt like slamming her to the floor, but that fuck-nigga shit wasn't in me. There was no way I was going to hurt a pregnant woman, especially one pregnant with my seed. Even killas had to draw the line somewhere. So, I held her until she calmed down. I could feel my phone vibrating in my pocket.

"Jahmani, if you don't let me go, I'm about to get on some petty shit and scream. Now, let me go. I'm leaving this city tonight."

I picked her up and tossed her on the bed. "Where the fuck you think you finna go wit' my baby in you, Ari? Huh?"

She brushed her hair out of her face. "Nigga, I don't know, but I ain't staying here. I refuse to sit around like a side bitch for only God knows how much longer. What do you expect me to do, Jahmani?" She scooted out of the bed and packed the last of her things into her suitcase, grabbed it up, and headed toward the door.

I jumped in her way. "Ari, shawty, what do you want me to do? I'm not trying to lose you like this. I'm still crazy about you, and we're about to have a baby together. What do you need for me to do?"

She shook her head and placed her hand over her forehead. "I don't know, Jahmani. There really is nothing you can do. We're on the run for murder. On top of that, Beans is gunning for us, as well as Linx. All I know is New York, but if I return there, all hell is sure to break loose. I'm so lost I'm thinking of going to any random city and starting over."

"You ain't gotta do that. I feel like we need to come up with a plan on what we're about to do. I know you're feeling some type of way because of Misty and I's relationship, but we need to focus on what's more important, which is our child. If you can give me one week, I'll have enough bread to move you out of this hotel and into any place you want so you can be comfortable. All I need is for you to chill one more week. That's it."

"And during this week, who are you going to be laid up with? Her or me?"

"Come on wit' that shit, Ari. Why you trying to cause all of this drama? You see who I'm fucking wit'. I'm wit' her now. That's what it is."

"Oh yeah? Well, Jahmani, you can kiss my ass. You and my cousin. My fuckin' cousin. Does that make any sense to you? You could've went and fucked wit' any bitch in the world, but you go and fuck wit' my cousin. You'sa trifling-ass negro. One of these days you gon' surely reap what you've sown. I don't know how, but the universe gon' get yo' ass back. Trust me on this." She sat on the edge of the bed and smiled. "Yeah, karma is a bitch. But you know what, Jahmani?

I'm stuck. I ain't got nowhere to go. So g'on 'head and leave. When you come back, my stupid ass'll be right here waiting for you. Why? 'Cause I put myself in this fucked-up position. Any woman who places all of her trust in a man is stupid. Any woman who gives a man all of her power is only setting herself up for destruction. Power is never meant to be given away. It's meant to be maintained and increased, especially when it comes to a woman. I placed myself in this predicament, so I'ma figure some thangs out. But g'on, I'll be here when you get back. That's how you got it set up anyway, right?"

I stepped in front of her and pulled her arm until she was standing in front of me. "I don't know how many times I am going to have to apologize to you, but if I have to do it a million times, I will. I'm sorry for everything I've taken you through. I'm sorry for us being in such a screwed-up position. I'm sorry for being with Misty, and I'm sorry about your people. I wish I could turn back the hands of time, but I can't. I can only be better from this day forth. Regardless to what you're thinking right now, I really do care about you. I always have, and I always will. I know we'll figure this shit out so we're both happy. Ain't no sense in us beefing. Now, all I need is for you to chill for a few days. Let me bust a few moves, and I'ma be right back to you. Can you do that?"

She ignored me for a full minute. My phone continued to buzz in my pocket.

She looked up to me and smiled. "Sure, honey. I'll be here when you get back, just like a good girl." She rolled her eyes and pushed me out of her face. "Nigga, do what you gotta do. You got one week. If you don't get us right by then, I'ma figure some things out on my own. Tell Misty I said this shit ain't over. She ain't never beat me in nothing, and she never will." She grabbed her Bible out of the drawer and opened it.

Ghost

***

When I slid back into Stephan's truck, he had a dumb-ass look on his face. "Nigga, you had me waiting on yo ass for three hours. What the fuck type of shit is that?"

I held my silence for a li'l while. I was replaying everything over in my head that had transpired with Ari, everything that took place and everything she said. A bunch of that shit didn't sit right wit' me. It was weighing heavy on my spirit.

Stephan pulled out of the parking lot. "Kid, somebody drop you off somewhere and you tell them you're going to be back at a specific time, you should be on time. I got my moms and Misty blowing me up like crazy. Damn."

I sat back in the seat and exhaled. "That's my bad, bruh. I was up there trying to get an understanding wit' somebody. Shit ran over. That's on me, though."

He sighed. "It's good, homie. Shit happens. While you was up there, I came upon another move, though. One I think gon' be right up yo' alley. You 'bout chopping some shit down?"

I nodded. "The way I'm feeling right now, it's the only thing I feel like doing."

Stephan nodded. "Then it's on, Bronx kid. Let's turn up.

Chapter 12

"Now, where the hell are you getting ready to go, Jahmani?" Misty snapped, following me around the room.

I threw a black t-shirt over my vest and put on my black Army fatigue jacket. I already had the black leather Timbs waiting by the door. Stephan told me I needed to be ready to get down for the cause, and I was trying my best to get into that mind frame, but Misty was getting on my last fuckin' nerve.

"Daddy, are you going to answer me? Why are you treating me so cold?" She hugged my body.

Damn, that shit melted me right away. I sighed and took her little arms from around me, looking into her beautiful face that appeared worried and afraid. "Baby, I gotta go out and bust this move with Stephan. It should be almost a hunnit bands. That's where I'm getting ready to go. I apologize for ignoring you." I kissed her forehead and went back to getting myself together.

"But you been gone all day, daddy. I been missing you all freaking day, now you're about to leave again. It's not fair."

Even though I knew Vicki was gon' feel some type of way, I still slid my feet into my Timbs and laced them just right. I was a New York nigga. We ain't believe in having our boots tied all tight and shit. It was all about being stylish. Even though I was going on a mission, that swagger shit was still in me. "Baby, I went over to holler at Ari, and shawty was just saying a bunch of shit that's fuckin' wit' my head, that's all. I'm trying to clear my mind before I go out there and get on this move. That's all."

She grabbed my chin and pushed it backward. "What the fuck is these, Jahmani?" She rubbed all over my neck. "You let this bitch suck all over your fuckin' neck. Really?" she snapped. She mugged me with seething anger. "How could you?"

I squeezed my eyelids together and stepped in front of the mirror, held my neck back, and saw the damage Ari had done. Sure enough, there we're three nice-sized hickeys on my neck. "You gotta be fuckin' kidding me," I whispered to myself.

"How was it?" Misty asked, stepping beside me and meeting my eyes in the mirror. "How fuckin' was it, Jahmani?"

I didn't even give her a response. I didn't feel like arguing or explaining myself. There was no way she was going to believe Ari and I hadn't slept together, so there was no use. Besides, I was tired of all the back-and-forth, anyway. I was in a far-away city I didn't know nothing about, about to hit a lick with a cat I barely knew with the weight of the world on my shoulders. I ain't have time for all of the drama.

I zipped up by fatigue coat and brushed past her. "Yo, we'll talk about that shit when I get home tonight. Give Lonnie a bath, and make sure she eat some kind of vegetables. She been avoiding them joints for the longest."

After those words was out, the last vision I had of Misty was her standing in he middle of the room with both fists balled.

***

I sat in the back of the makeshift casino with Stephan, looking around and trying my best to analyze what was going on around me. The casino was definitely back-alley. It consisted of a few roulette wheels, black jack tables, and three crap-shooting slots. Most of the dealers were old heads. The crowd appeared to be mixed in age, though. The sounds of The Temptations crooned out of the speakers. The casino was dimly lit except for the places where the gambling took place. An older woman about the age of 55 came over to our table and sat a bottle of VSOP on top of it with two glasses before swishing away.

Stephan smiled. "This muthafucka is a gold mine right here, Jahmani. Would you believe these old heads pull in almost two million dollars a weekend?" He filled the two glasses with liquor and pushed one over to me.

I picked it up and downed it. I really didn't fuck wit' VSOP like that, but I needed something to take the edge off. My body was feeling funny. I didn't know why. "Two million? What the fuck they got going on in here?"

Stephan downed his first glass of liquor and poured himself another. "All type of shit. The gambling is just a front for so many other things. This muthafucka ran by this old head called Sam. Sam used to be a pimp back in the day, and his father was into long-sharking and gambling real tough. Long story short, the legend goes that Sam's father was connected to Bugsy Siegel, and Bugsy wound up giving him a few casinos like the one we're in now. Not any good ones, only the ones that would pass as a casino so Bugsy could use it as a post to run his dope and guns through. You see, since day one the Italians have kicked and chosen which black folk they were going to uplift and invest in all for the greater good of themselves. Sam's people are able to live the high life while they are used as a distributing post to corrupt our community, amongst other things. This shit been going on for years, and it's a long story I don't feel like getting into." He took another shot of liquor.

"Yeah, and one I don't feel like hearing. I wanna know why we're here." I looked around and saw a thick-ass dark-skinned broad walk past with a tray full of bills. She winked at Stephan, dropped a wallet-like thing, and kept it moving.

He smiled. "Tonight, we about to hit they ass before they can ship the money they've made all week up the coast to The Siegel's." Stephan eased from the table and recovered the wallet, placed it inside his jacket, and slid back into our booth.

I peeped the dark-skinned broad from the corner of my eye. She waited in front of some metal gate before it buzzed. She stepped inside of it and disappeared. "I take it you got shawty ass on deck?"

He laughed. "Yo, that's my cousin right there. Shawty from Baltimore, along with myself, but she been working down here in Greenville for the last eighteen months. Sam bitch-ass got a thang for her. A thang that's gon' wind up getting his ass in a world of trouble."

Another older woman strolled through with a tray full of cash. She stood in front of the same gate, waited until it buzzed, and entered. "Yo, son, what goes on back there?"

Stephan poured himself another drink. "That's where they count the profits. It's about ten bitches back there that count the money. After they finish counting, they send the totals upstairs to Sam by a dumbwaiter. It travels right upstairs into his office. Once it gets there, he has a six-foot safe. That bitch full of cash and all type of product. Son moving and grooving, and he even got his hand in twelve's pockets."

I continued to scan the area. "That's what's up. But my next question to you is how are we about to lay this bitch down? We been sitting here for almost an hour. I see one, two, three, four cameras, and I can only imagine they had a few of them trained on the parking lot when we rolled up, so what are you seeing here?"

He laughed. "Don't pay no attention to all that shit. Just pay attention to the pussy that's around here. Pussy make the muthafuckin' world go round. Long as you can control another man's pussy, you can control and destruct his whole operation." He sipped out of the glass and slid from the booth. "Let's roll out. It's time."

The dark-skinned female came past again, and we followed her into the hallway to the bathrooms. She looked behind her, then both ways before she stepped into the women's room and pulled Stephan in beside her. I followed, as well.

"Huh, here go the key to the back way to his office. I been keeping track of the totals. He should have one point two million in the safe upstairs and five hundred thousand he's currently confirming. Now, the office is wired for gunfire detection. If you guys let off any shots up there, an alarm will be triggered that goes straight to the fourth district station. You'll have so many badges around this casino that you won't be able to get away."

Stephan shrugged his shoulders. "That's cool. That's why I got these." He held up two silenced .380s and handed me one. "They can't detect what they don't hear. Anything else we need to know, Caryn?"

She shook her head. "Nall, that's all I can think of. Wait a few minutes and let me stroll back out, then take the back way. Remember, right by the exit sign is a hook in the wall. Jiggle it and slide the beige portion to the side. Fit that key into the lock and swipe that card inside the wallet I gave you, and you'll be good. I love you, Stephan."

She stepped over to him and he snatched her up, grabbed her ass, and tongued her down for thirty seconds. I mean, his fingers went all the way under her backside into her crease. I knew because she was rocking this short skirt, and it managed to rise onto her waist. I watched his fingers play over one of the brown lips. Her pussy looked good.

They broke the kiss and she stepped back, breathing hard. Her nipples poked through her white top. "Damn, cuz, you always all over me. Let me get out of this bathroom before that fool get to searching the camera to see where I am." She eased into the hallway and allowed the door to close.

Stephan adjusted his piece. "Shawty somethin' else." He placed the gun in the small of his back. "You ready to handle this bidness?"

Hell yeah, I was. I also couldn't wait to get back to Vicki's crib so I could get me some pussy. Seeing them do their thing affected me like crazy. "Yeah, let's do this."

***

Stephan stepped to the side and allowed me to slip past him into the narrow space that led to Sam's office. It smelled funny inside the wall, like paint thinner and peppermint. I saw more than a few mice scurrying by on the floor as we traveled to his office, but they didn't bother me. In my opinion, they were poor excuses for mice. I was accustomed to big-ass raccoon-sized mice. Those were the kind we had in New York. Them bitches were so big they hunted cats.

We came outside of Sam's door. It read "MANAGER" across it. Stephan placed his hand on the handle and lowered his eyes. He held the gun by the side of his head and nodded at me. "One, two, three!" He threw open the door.

I rushed in with the .380 aimed forward. The first sight was of what I assumed to be Sam sitting at the desk with a bundle of cash in his hand. He had an earpiece in his ear and money all over the desk. He was dark-skinned with a gray afro and a goatee.

"Aw, shit, Joe! It's a hit. It's a hit. I'm being robbed!" he hollered into the earpiece.

I reached across the desk and punched him as hard as I could. I mean, I hit his ass so hard he flew backward into the wall. I jumped on the desk, and hopped off it, pulled him up, and ripped the earpiece from his ear. "Shut the fuck up." I backhanded him as hard as I could and dropped him again.

Stephan pulled a black plastic bag out of his drawers and started to dump the cash inside it. "Unlock the safe, Sam. We ain't finna play wit' you."

Sam winced in my grip. "I can't do that. Bugsy's boys'll kill me."

I snatched him all the way up and slammed him into the wall, placing the .380 on his right eye socket. "Negro, if you don't, then I'ma blow ya head off. Now, turn yo' monkey-ass around and open the safe."

He swallowed. I watched his Adam's apple go up and down. "Okay. Okay. Just, please, don't kill me."

He turned around and began to fiddle with the digital safe while Stephan finished cleaning the money off the table. Stephan came and stood beside me. "Hurry up, Sam, and don't try none of them old school tricks. I'm wise to yo' shit."

I didn't know what he meant, and I didn't care. The way I saw it, we had a limited amount of time to get out of there before whoever this Joe stud was came to help. I placed the silenced barrel to the back of Sam's thigh and leaned into his ear. "Nigga, you got three seconds."

"Okay. Okay. I'm moving as fast as I can." He seemed to speed up, pressing in a series if numbers on the digital keypad, before pausing. "Fellas, are you sure there isn't anything we can work out?" he started.

Zoof.

The gun jumped in my hand as the bullet shot through the chamber and wound up putting a huge hole in the back of his thigh. He fell onto Stephan and hollered as loud as he could, it seemed.

Stephan threw him into the safe. "Open it."

He hopped up and down on his off leg and finally opened the safe before falling to his ass crying tears of agony. He looked pathetic. I'd always hated to see grown men cry, no matter the circumstances.

Stephan went around the office emptying the recorders, and then he was standing next to me, filling his bag with money. "We gotta hurry up and get out of here, Jahmani."

I took every crumb he missed, tied my double bag into knots, and stopped in front of the door. "What we gon' do about him? That fool seen our faces." I needed to know. I already had a buncha shit on my plate. I didn't need a whole other problem.

Stephan waved him off. "That old fool know what's good. He live by the code of the streets. He ain't no rat. Let's get out of here." He rushed past me into the hallway.

I mugged the old dude for a long time. He remained curled in a ball, whimpering. Something told me to body his ass. I felt it deep in my gut.

I heard sirens somewhere close, second-guessed myself, and took off running behind Stephan.

Chapter 13

They shut the city of Greenville down for six straight days. I mean, they were shaking down and pulling over everybody in the district. If a person looked like they fit myself and Stephan's description, their ass was hauled in. Every day that passed I regretted not smoking Sam. I should have went with my first mind and instincts. Every time I passed Stephan in the hallway; all he could do was apologize for his poor choice to leave that fool alive.

We came away with one point seven million dollars in cash. Six hundred thousand was take-home for me. I honestly didn't care what Stephan did with the rest of the money. He was saying he had to hit his cousin and a few other people for putting the lick together, and I didn't stress the fact. Six hunnit bands was a nice come-up. That put me well past my quota of five hundred racks, so I was mentally trying to figure out my next move and what part of the country we should roll out to when I had got a call from Ari on the seventh day after we'd hit the lick.

I was sitting in the living room, hugged up with Lonnie and Misty watching *Ralph Breaks the Internet,* when the phone buzzed. Misty mugged me and looked down at it, then grabbed the popcorn and set it on her lap. "G'on. see who that is in the other room, Jahmani. I'll get on yo' ass later. I don't feel like arguing right now. Bye." She flared her nostrils and wrapped her arm around Lonnie's shoulder.

I got up and answered the phone. "What's good, Ari?"

She was quiet at first. "What do you mean, 'what's good'? It's day seven. What are we going to do?"

I covered the receiver as Vicki walked past in a pair of white spandex shorts that had her ass sitting right. She locked eyes with me and licked her lips. "Hey, baby, you alright?"

My eyes trailed down to that ass. I didn't care if she knew. "Yeah, aunty, but when me and you gon' spend some time together so I can get to know you better?" My eyes sized her up, stopping on her hard nipples that were jutting out of her white beater.

She smiled. "Boy, you ain't nothin' but trouble. You don't thank I see you peeping all this ass back there?" She turned around to face me.

Her shorts were all up in her gap. I could make out both pussy lips. My dick got super hard. I wanted some of that vet pussy bad. I was thirsty for some. "I don't mean no disrespect, but you just so damn bad Ms. Vicki. You do something to me."

She laughed and walked off with her cheeks jiggling like Jell-O. "Nall, baby, you want me to do something to you."

I watched that ass until it disappeared. My dick was jumping up and down in my pants. I needed some relief bad.

When I placed the phone back to my ear, there was nothing but a dial tone. I called Ari's number back a few times before she picked up with a sigh. "Yo, why you hang up?"

"Don't play wit' me. You thought I was about to sit around and wait for you until you decided you wanted to talk? Boy, please. What we finna do, man?"

I adjusted my piece. It was still throbbing like crazy after seeing Vicki in those spandex shorts. "I got a nice amount of bread now, so I can get you right. I'ma come and scoop you in a few hours. Be ready to go."

"Ready to go where?" Ari questioned.

That was a good one, because I didn't have any idea myself. "I don't know. I kinda wanna get you and Misty in the same room so y'all can come to an understanding. Sooner or later we gon' all have to travel together, so y'all might as well nip all of those animosities in the bud right now."

Ari scoffed into the phone. "What is your end game here,

Jahmani? What you thinking? You finna be able to have both of your hoez under the same roof like you some type of boss Mack or something? If that's what you thinking, let me just tell you right now that ain't about to happen."

"Ari, I ain't even thought that far into things. As a start, I want y'all to get an understanding. Can you do that?"

"I guess. I really don't see what there is to get an understanding about, but whatever. I'll be waiting for y'all to get here." She hung up the phone.

I tried to gather myself. I could already see my day was headed for the worse, but the good thing was Ari had agreed to have a sit-down with myself and Misty. Now all I had to do was get Misty on board. It was time for us to leave North Carolina, and I didn't plan on leaving neither girl behind. We had to travel to the next destination together. In order to do so, we would have to all be on the same page.

I stuck my head into the living room and motioned with my finger for Misty to come to me. She got up front the couch and kissed Lonnie on the forehead. "I'll be right back, baby. I just want to see what your uncle wants."

Lonnie was so engrossed in the movie that she acted as if she didn't even hear her.

Misty stepped into the hallway and in front of me. "What's up, baby?"

"Yo, I want you to roll out wit' me somewhere." I took ahold of her hand and led her toward the stairs.

She pulled back against me. "Wait, wait, wait. Where am I going?"

"Just about ten minutes away. I want you to talk to somebody." I started toward the stairs with her in front of me.

She slouched her shoulders. "Daddy, I don't wanna go nowhere. I'm chilling in my sweats. I just wanna watch Disney and Pixar movies with Lonnie all day and feel like a kid again.

You can go meet these people all by yourself as soon as you tell me who they are." She stopped in front of our room, and blocked my path from coming in. "So, who are you going to see?"

"Ari."

She frowned and crossed her arms in front of her body. "I should've known. You know what? Just let me get dressed. I'll be ready to go in a minute. You can wait for me in the car. I'ma make sure Vicki will keep an eye on Lonnie, and then I'll meet you in the car.

"Baby, I –"

She held up her hand to stop me. "Don't say another word to me until we get there. I'm so frustrated with you right now that I can't even think straight."

***

Ari was the first one to jump out of the car as soon as I pulled into the lakefront. It was ninety degrees outside once again, hot and humid. The beach was packed, so I chose to park in a section of the park where there were mostly deserted picnic tables. Ari got out of the car, walked up to a bunch of rocks, and picked one up. She tossed it into the water, then picked up another one.

Misty's hair blew in the wind. She stepped closer to me and reached for my hand. "Jahmani, don't get to acting all funny around this bitch. I swear to God, I'll make both of y'all whoop my ass, 'cause I ain't going. You belong to me. It's us. This just what it is. Let her know that and it'll save her a whole lot of heartache and pain down the road. Let's go."

I scanned the area in search of any potential threats. After seeing none, I continued on my path. We made it beside Ari a few moments later. I didn't know how things were going to go, but I was about to see.

Ari skipped a rock across the water. She smiled and removed a strand of hair from her face. Her dark caramel skin glistened in the sunlight. I could smell her perfume drifting from her body. She looked as beautiful as the first time I'd seen her in my mother's church.

"This the first time I really been out of that cramped hotel since I been in North Carolina. The fresh air feels good to me." She skipped another rock.

Misty turned her back to the lakefront. "Alright, we here. What's good, Jahmani? What we supposed to be discussing?"

"He probably wanna tell you first and foremost that I'm pregnant with his baby. And secondly, he want all of us to live together in peace and harmony." She laughed and threw another rock into the water.

Misty's face screwed into a ball. "She's pregnant by you? Since when?"

"Since three months," Ari added. "That's the only reason I ain't whooping yo' ass right now. You already know you can't fuck wit' my bidness. I been whooping yo' ass all of our lives."

Misty sidestepped her comments. She pushed me. "So, she's pregnant? When were you going to tell me this? Huh?" She pushed me again. "I'm talking to you. When?"

I blocked her li'l hands and turned her around, pulled her to my body, and hugged her li'l ass. "Yo, calm yo' ass down. I ain't tell you about it because I still ain't got no confirmation. I mean, she told me she was pregnant, but she ain't shown me no proof. I'm still waiting on that."

"That's how you gon' play shit, Jahmani?" Now she was on the side of my face. "What the fuck do I have to gain by lying to you, huh? Ain't shit changed since I told you I was pregnant. You still all up this bitch's ass," she snapped.

Misty tried her best to break my hold. "Ari, get the fuck out of my daddy's face. Daddy, let me go!"

"Daddy? Yo, you got my cousin calling you 'daddy' and shit? Y'all done took it there?" Ari shouted, stepping in front of Misty. "You know yo' history wit' yo' pops, and this is what you calling him? You ain't nothing but a red ho."

"Daddy, fuck this. Let me whoop this bitch. She think it's sweet. I owe her ass for all the shit she did to me as a kid, anyway. Let me go!" Misty twisted from right to left. She slumped down in my arms. Her shirt rose to reveal her bra and stomach.

Ari stepped back and took off her earrings. "Bitch, ain't no hoez over here. I done whooped you before, I don't mind doing it again. Let that red bitch go and I'ma shake her like a red nose. Bronx-style."

Misty twisted out of my grasp and hopped up. She pulled her long, curly hair back into a ponytail and then a bun. "I used to be scared of you when I was little. That's why I let you and your sick-ass brother do all that shit to me, but I'm grown now, bitch. I found my voice, and I ain't going. You think you finna have a baby by my daddy, you done lost yo' fuckin' mind. Ain't nobody finna take him away from me." She removed her earrings and cracked her knuckles.

Ari laughed. "You doing all that shit for what? You ain't 'bout this action. But since you think you is, let's rock." She balled up her fists and held her guards up.

Misty lowered her chin and protected it with a fist on each side. She took a deep breath and lunged forward, swung, and caught Ari right on the bottom lip, busting it. Ari flew backward and tried to catch her balance, but before she had the chance to, Misty was all over her. Misty swung wild and connected with every other blow, it seemed.

Ari wound up on her knees with her head covered. "Aw,

bitch, let me up. Let me up. You ain't on shit. Just let me up."

Misty took a few paces backward and waved her to get up. "Come on. Get up. What's taking you so long?" She rolled her head around on her neck.

A crowd of people rushed over and surrounded us. They chanted, "Fight. Fight. Fight."

Ari stood up and shot daggers at me. "This what you wanna see, Jahmani, huh? You like seeing two cousins fighting over yo' ass? And after all you've taken me through?" she cried.

Misty rushed her. "Ain't no sense in crying, bitch. It's on." She windmilled her with punches, but this time Ari was ready. She blocked the first two and returned four of her own. One busted Misty's nose. Then they were on the ground, rolling around in the dirt like animals. First Misty would be on top, catching Ari again and again, and then they would switch positions.

This lasted for about five minutes before I pulled them apart. Both women were breathing hard by that point.

Ari took off running to the car. "Jahmani, drop me back off at the hotel! Now!"

Ghost

Chapter 14

After dropping Ari back off at the hotel, me and Misty wound up back at Vicki's home. She slammed the door to the car as hard as she could. "Fuck! I'm tired of this shit, Jahmani!" Her dress was ripped. Her nose bled. Her hair was a mess. "I can't believe you kept that shit from me. I been one hunnit to you ever since you and I have been messing around together." She stormed away and headed toward the back of the house. "Come into the backyard. Now, Jahmani!"

I ran my hand over my waves and wanted to scream. They were both driving me crazy. I followed her to the back as a text came though on my phone from Ari. It read: "*It's good, Jahmani. You can have her. I got both of y'all asses. Just watch. You ain't even ask me if I was okay. Nigga, I'm pregnant wit' yo' kid! Reap what you sow, though. You'll see!*"

I put my phone in my pocket. When I got to the backyard, Misty was pacing back and forth and talking to herself. I watched her dab her fingers at the corner of her mouth, then she looked at them and wiped the blood on her dress.

"Misty, baby, can you calm down for me?" I made my way over to her. I wanted to wrap her in my arms. I figured if I could wrap her in my arms, then I could put that affection on her ass, and that would cause her to calm down.

"Jahmani, right now I don't want to hear your mouth. Ain't nothing you about to say gon' be able to stop me from feeling like I'm feeling. That bitch is pregnant, and you ain't told me shit. That's technical foul. You're super bogus, and you know it." She glared at me with her fist balled.

I had to do some kind of damage control. I didn't like lying to nobody. I had always been an upfront type of dude, but I couldn't have my li'l woman fuming the way she was. We needed to move out of North Carolina, and I needed her by my side. I could tell Lonnie had taken a major liking to her. To disrupt their relationship at this juncture would only hurt my niece. In addition to that truth, I was feeling some type of way about her as well. Misty had taken a major portion of my heart, as much as I wanted to admit it.

"Yo, she ain't even say nothin' about her being pregnant until this morning. That's one of the reasons why I wanted to get us all together. I wanted her to admit what she told me in front of both of us. I knew you would see through that shit. Then she hollering she three months, and her stomach flat as hell. I don't believe that shit, Misty. I swear I don't. She just trying to break us up."

Misty wiped a tear away from her right eye. "She only told you that today?"

I stepped to her and held her shoulders. "Yeah, baby, and it was only after I told her I wasn't fucking wit' her on that level no more. I swear on my niece that her and I ain't gotten down ever since you and I have."

Misty thought about this for a minute. She allowed me to rub her face, to wipe her tears away, but when I tried to pull her into my warm embrace for a hug, she pushed me away.

"Wait a minute. Jahmani, I saw the passion marks on your neck the other day. You stayed out all night one night and didn't come home until the afternoon. That bitch is staying in a hotel. There is only one bed there. You mean to tell me you want me to believe y'all ain't fucked? Nigga, you out of your mind, and you know it." She said this while pointing at me with her pinky finger. "Y'all been doing something, and it sucks I can't even trust you when I'm supposed to be able to. I been riding by your side ever since we crossed over to one another. Damn, this hurts." She turned her back to me and covered her face. When she removed her hands, her face was wet wit' tears.

I snatched her ass up and wrapped her in my arms. She struggled to break free of the hold. "Baby, I swear to you on my niece that her and I ain't gotten down ever since you and I been together. I wouldn't do you like that. I love yo' li'l crazy ass. My word is bond. Now, you need to chill. We sitting out here beefing for nothing. Please, listen to me." Every killa had a weakness, and Misty had become mine. I honestly didn't like seeing her cry. I didn't like her feeling betrayed. I didn't like her feeling alone and vulnerable. I loved this woman, and I knew for a fact there was nothing I wouldn't do for her or about her. I had to be better for her. I held her tighter.

"Daddy, I don't want her to have your kid. I don't want you connected to that bitch more than you already are. I swear, I hope she's lying. I know how conniving and vindictive she is. I just pray this is one of her ploys to try and keep you bound. I mean, I'd ride with you through anything, but if she's having your child, I honestly don't know what I would do. Yeah, she was before me, and I should respect whatever happened before me, especially since our coming to be is a bit controversial but dealing with Ari for the next eighteen years could not be healthy for nobody. That bitch is trickier than a magician." She broke my hold and faced me. "You bet not never keep nothing like that from me ever again. I don't care what you're thinking or what time you think will be the right time. As a woman, you are to give me my due. Respect me enough to tell me things right away and give me the right to decide if I want to stay and handle them or not. It's not fair for you to decide everything. Do you understand me, daddy?"

"I do, baby. I swear I do, and I'm sorry. I should've told you as soon as I knew. I just didn't know how to. But from here on out, anytime it's something as severe as that, I will tell you about it right away. I promise."

"Well, it shouldn't be nothing that pops off as severe as

that anymore. You're supposed to love me unconditionally, just like I do you. And if that's the case, then you won't be getting nobody else pregnant." She lowered her head and sighed. "With all of this bullshit going on, it has kind of spoiled what I wanted to tell you about us. Jahmani, unlike that bitch and her lies, I wanted to let you know we are pregnant for real. I peed on two sticks this morning, and they were both positive. And I did the same thing yesterday, and they were positive as well. We're going to have a baby. You and I. Me and my daddy. How does that make you feel?"

I stood there for a moment to allow that to process inside my mind. I imagined what life would be like with her as my wife and the mother of my child, and I couldn't stop smiling. I pulled her into my arms again and planted kisses all over her face. "You was keeping a secret from me, too," I teased. "You should've told me yesterday." More kisses.

She started cracking up. "Get off of me, daddy. I'm still mad at you. Get off of me." Though she said this, she made very little effort to fight me off. She was too busy laughing and getting loved up.

Vicki stuck her head out the backdoor. "I take it you two are good now?" She looked from Misty back to me.

We nodded.

"Well, good. I cooked a lot of food, and I want us to enjoy it. Y'all come on inside and wash up. Come on now." She waved us in.

***

That night I tossed and turned in the bed. I couldn't sleep. I kept trying to figure out what I was going to do with two children on the way while being on the run. I didn't know if Ari was really pregnant, but I really wanted to find out. If she was going to have my child, then I needed to be there for her. We had to come to an understanding, not solely for ourselves, but for the child most importantly. I didn't need to be sexually involved with her in order to be there for my kid. I could tell from the moment I dropped her back off at the hotel and didn't walk her upstairs there was going to be bad blood between us. I needed to make things right. After all, the bickering and fighting was all because of me.

So, I tossed and turned about that and the fact I felt so vengeful in my heart. I needed to clap back at Beans. I needed to find that fool Linx and get at him. Samantha also weighed heavy on my heart. I wondered what was good wit' her?

It took me nearly three hours to fall into a light sleep. Just as I was starting to dream, Misty woke me up by pushing on my chest. I opened my eyes to a blurry vision of her. "Yo, what's good, ma?"

"Shh, daddy, my aunty Vicki trying to get down wit' us. She got some of that brandy in her system, and she won't stop feeling all over me, she got me horny as fuck. Come on, let's go downstairs to the living room real quick. Stephan ain't here." She reached under the covers and squeezed my dick."

I just knew I had to be dreaming. I pinched myself and felt the pain. "Yo, you serious?" I sat up.

Misty stroked my dick and kissed the head, sucked me into her mouth for a second, and then popped it back out. "Yeah, daddy. Look," she moaned, directing my vision with her head.

I glanced toward the doorway and saw Vicki standing there with her pink silk robe wide open. She wore a white negligee underneath it. It was so short I could make out the bottom portion of her sex lips.

"Yo, y'all serious? We ain't gotta go downstairs. We can stay right in here."

Vicki slowly walked across the fluffy carpet in bare feet.

When she got beside the bed, she rubbed my chest. "Welcome to the south, Jahmani. We about to blow yo' mind. Misty, you sho he can handle what we about to do to him?" she asked, sending her fingers through Misty's hair and pulling her head off my dick.

Misty breathed hard. "Yeah, aunty. He can handle it. Jahmani don't know it, but he got that weird shit in him, too. Ever since he heard you and Stephan going at it, he ain't been able to take his eyes off of you. He think he slick." She stroked me faster.

Vicki crawled into the bed beside Misty, her ass in the air. The negligee rose to show her peach from the back. It was lightly shaven. The lips were thick and partially opened, just enough to show me a hint of pink. Her thick thighs opened as I rubbed into her gap. She moaned. "Un, baby. What, you wanna be my son, too?"

I sucked two fingers into my mouth and slid them into her box, ran them in and out until she was soaking wet. Her cream seeped out of her pinkness and dripped down her inner thighs. I slipped from my back and stuck my head between her legs, licking all the way up from her knee to her hipbone. She tasted a bit salty and, oh, so forbidden. Even though she wasn't nothing to me, I was trying to put myself inside of Stephan's mind frame. I was on my taboo shit, and I had to have that ass.

Her and Misty made out. They held each other by the face while their tongues wrestled. I watched Misty squeeze Vicki's titties through her negligee. Vicki rubbed all over Misty's ass after hiking her shirt skirt up to her waist. Her fingers played over Misty's cleft, then she was two fingers deep inside of her, sucking on her neck loudly.

I ran my tongue in circles around Vicki's ass and fingered her hot pussy fast. The lips were like suction, and they tried to trap my digits inside her body. I stroked my piece and got him ready to go. I wanted to fuck her thick ass bad.

Misty lay on her back and opened her thighs wide. She spread her lips for Vicki. "Come on, aunty. You know what I want."

Vicki groaned and lowered her face inside of Misty's thighs. Then she was eating away. Her head went from side-to-side while she held her tongue out. She slurped and licked.

Misty threw her head back. "Fuck her, daddy. Hit that pussy. It's okay. Long as I'm in the same room, it's okay."

I grabbed ahold of her hips and slid in. As soon as my piece got halfway into her furnace, I began to shake like crazy. Her shit felt so cushiony. I slammed balls deep and rested against all of that ass, whimpering like a li'l chump or something. She worked them vet walls, and it felt like she was massaging me with her fist.

I licked along her spine. "I'm finna fuck this pussy, mama."

She shivered. "Uh, baby, don't say that to me. I can't handle that talk." She pushed back again.

I stood tall on my knees and watched our connection. Her brown lips wrapped around my dick looked good to me. I had a thing for older women, and Vicki was the epitome of a fine-ass older woman. I held onto that waist and got to fuckin' her hard, with no mercy. She was too thick for mercy. I knew she could handle this muthafucka.

Bam. Bam. Bam. Bam.

Deeper, and faster. Every time our skins crashed into one another, her ass would jiggle along with her thighs. Her pussy slurped at me.

Misty wrapped her thighs around Vicki's face. She humped upward from the bed, riding her face like a true slut. "Pipe her, daddy. Pipe her, daddy. Un. Daddy. Pipe her. Un, Vicki, I'm cumming already. I'm cumming already." She rode her face with her mouth wide open. She looked so fine it was ridiculous.

Vicki continued to lick from side-to-side. As Misty got to shaking like crazy, her head became still. Misty screamed and came all over her face.

I yanked Vicki away and forced her knees to her shoulders, lying back on top of her. As soon as I slid through her fortress, I got to pounding her thick ass out with no mercy. Misty crawled over and sucked my neck. She kissed my chest and placed her face between Vicki and my sexing parts. Her ass was in the air now, so as I fucked Vicki, I fingered her li'l box. This drove her crazy.

"Uh. Uh. Uh. Baby. Ooh, shit. Ooh, shit, Jahmani. Cum in mama. Cum in me, baby. Aw, fuck!" She dug her nails into my forearms and came hard. Her walls clenched at me. The feeling of her body demanding my release brought forth my climax. I forced her strapped ass into a ball, and came back-to-back, jerking on top of her biting her neck.

As soon as I pulled out, Misty was between her thighs, cleaning up our sexual residue. I rubbed all over her ass and fell to my back. She lay next to me and tongued me down. "I love you, daddy. I love you so much."

Vicki eased out of the bed and picked up her robe from the floor before stepping into the hallway and closing the door behind her. I didn't know what that whole thing was all about, but I was glad I got a chance to see what Vicki's box was like.

Chapter 15

"Nah, son, fuck that. Them niggas caught me slipping for fifteen bands, my nigga. I ain't about to roll over and let that shit ride. Kid an' 'em just think it's sweet. You finna ride over there wit' me or what?" Stephan asked after pulling me into the den.

His clothes were all ripped and dirty. He looked like he'd just gotten his ass whooped. I ain't feel like getting involved wit' his fool ass. I was tired from fucking wit' Vicki and Misty all night. Once Vicki left the room, Misty had jumped on top of me and rode my shit for two hours, reclaiming her territory. That pussy was so good I let her do her thing until my shit felt raw, then I pushed her li'l ass up off of me. I guess her seeing me with her aunty drove her crazy. She had that southern shit flowing through her veins, so I could only imagine. Either way, I was happy to be a part of the family. I could stay in the south forever.

I looked up at this dumbass nigga. "Yo, kid, where the fuck these niggas even at?" I was more than irritated, stretching my arms over my head and yawning. It was one o'clock in the afternoon.

"Son an' 'em rock over there off Jefferson Boulevard. They got a trap full of li'l niggas. It's about six of them jokers. All they do is pop pills and sip lean all day. If we roll through there at about ten or so tonight, we'll catch 'em in a slumber."

"How the fuck they catch you slipping, though? I though you was one of Baltimore's finest." I had to throw a slug at this clown. I ain't feel like jamming wit' him, no way. I wanted to take my ass to sleep.

"Fuck you mean? Nigga, I am Baltimore. We was shooting dice, and I was tearing they ass off. I hit, like, six sevens in a row. One of them punks got to talking about I was clutching the dice and not shaking them."

"Was you?" I asked, yawning again.

"Kid, that's neither here nor there. The bottom line is I was striking their ass, and they got salty. One of them stood up and waited until I rolled before he hit me on the back of the head with a forty-ounce bottle still in the brown paper bag. When he did that, they got to scraping me out. They took all of the money from the center of the pile and, like, eight gees from my pockets. Took my Glock and everything. I can't take this loss lying down, homie. I wanna go over there and put a few niggas in a coffin, you feel me?"

I lay back and closed my eyes. "Yo, I'm down for whatever, son, just as long as you let me catch a few zees first."

"That's cool wit' me. I wanna spend some time wit' my moms for a few hours, anyway. I'ma go and pick her up from work and take her out to eat. You know, spoil her a li'l bit. We should get back at around nine or so. That enough rest for you?"

I stood up and scratched my head, then rubbed the top of my waves. "That should be cool. I'm finna go find my baby girl right now and cuddle up wit' her li'l ass. I'ma get at you later."

He stood up and we gave each other half-hugs. He patted my back and disappeared out of the back of the house.

As soon as he stepped from the room, my phone buzzed, and Misty entered the den. "Daddy, I need you to hold me for a li'l while, my depression messing wit' me." She walked into my arms and hugged me.

I saw it was Ari hitting me up. I placed the phone to my ear. "Baby, this Ari. Don't be acting all weird and shit. I just wanna see what she want." I looked down at her.

She rolled her eyes and took a step back with her hands on her hips. "Make it quick. I'm not playing, either." Her nostrils flared. She looked angry and annoyed.

I laughed. "Yeah, a'ight. Hello?"

"Hello, Jahmani?"

"Yeah, what's good, shawty?"

"I need you to come to the hotel and chill wit' me for a minute. I don't feel too good." She took a deep breath and slowly exhaled to emphasize her point.

I mugged the phone before placing it back to my ear. "Are you serious?"

She was silent for a moment. "Yes, I'm serious. I need you for a few hours, then you can go back to her. I swear, I don't wanna fight no more. I know where we stand, and I'm cool wit' that. I just need a li'l care right now, that's all. Please, don't deny me. I am begging you."

"What that bitch saying, Jahmani?"

I held up a finger. "How soon do you need me to come over? I gotta handle some bidness tonight, but I can stroll through there first thing in the morning. You think you can manage until then?"

Misty looked heated. "You finna go over there again after what that bitch texted you? No, the fuck you ain't. I ain't finna allow it, Jahmani. You tell her to kiss yo' ass, and mine, too. Matter fact, give me this phone." She got to reaching for the phone all reckless, scratching at my arm.

I had the phone on mute. I pushed her li'l ass on the couch. "Baby, shut the fuck up! Alright? Sit yo' ass right there and don't say another fuckin' word. Let me handle this shit. You for that?"

She crossed her arms and looked off. "You ain't gotta be snapping on me for that bitch. You betta watch yo' tone." She continued to look away from me.

I was heated, sleepy, and very annoyed. "Yeah, whatever. Anyway." I took the phone. "Hello?"

"Yeah, let me guess. She ain't trying to hear you coming to me, huh?" Ari asked.

"Anyway, what if I come through tonight at about eleven or twelve?" I wanted to make sure Ari was good. I had a timetable in my head of leaving North Carolina in less than two weeks. Ari was going to have to come along until she was able to make further arrangements. I couldn't just leave her out on a limb like that. Besides, I had a couple boxes of pregnancy tests I wanted her to use in front of me.

"That sounds good, just as long as you really come, Jahmani. I'll make do. But are you really coming at that time tonight?"

"Yeah, I'll be there. You got my word on that."

"Alright then, I'll see you then. I love you, whether you believe it or not."

I didn't know what to believe. "Ari, I'll see you later, and we'll figure some things out then. Alright. Until later on, hold ya head." I disconnected the call.

Misty stood up and laughed. "You one of the most stupidest niggas I ever met in my life. I just don't get you. What would make you continue to pursue this bitch, knowing she's scorned?"

"I'm finna make her ass piss on a few of them pregnancy sticks. I wanna take her to the doctor to find out if she's really pregnant, but I'll take one step at a time. Trust me, I know what I'm doing." I eased past her.

"What you gon' do if you find out she is pregnant, huh? What, you about to be a father to both of our children? That it? You don't think you're going to have to choose eventually? Huh?"

"Shawty, shut the fuck up. Damn. You getting on my nerves," I snapped feeling my blood boil.

"I don't care about you getting irritated. This ain't just your life here. It's mines, our unborn child's, and then yours. You don't get to make all of the decisions. Screw that. I need to know what your game plan is. If it doesn't fit into my agenda, I'm leaving your ass tonight. I've had enough. Period."

I tilted my head toward the ceiling. I needed to get ahold of myself. I was seconds away from choking her ass out. "Misty, I love you, baby girl, but you are really testing my patience right now. I ain't get no sleep last night. Your cousin want me to bust a lick wit' him, then I gotta go over there to force this girl to piss on more than one pregnancy stick. I'm already exhausted. I am begging you to leave me the fuck alone right now."

She stepped into my glamour. "Nope. Not as long as I have this child growing inside of me. Not as long as you're swearing up and down that you love me, and not as long as my future hangs in the balance of whatever decision you're going to make. As long as all of this is in play, I'ma be all under your skin like a splinter. Now, tell me what's good?"

"Look, if I find out she really is pregnant, then I ain't got no choice other than to find out if it's mine. If it's my seed, then I'ma do everything I have to as a man to ensure the baby don't need or want for anything as long as I am alive. That's just that. That don't mean I'ma be with her. I am more than happy being with just you. You're all I care about. All I see."

She smacked her lips. "Now, you and I both know that is a damn lie. Boy, yo' eyes stay wandering. Hell, if I hadn't let you get some of Vicki, you would've found a way to get some of her on your own. That would've crushed me, so I chose to be a part of it rather than have you go behind my back. I got tired of hearing her tell me how fine you was, anyway. I knew where that shit was headed. But anyway, you g'on 'head and do what you gotta do tonight. I'm not going to stand in your way. That would be so petty of me to do so. However, just to let you know, my gut is telling me you are making a huge mistake. I keep telling you that bitch is going to be the death of you, but you won't listen, and I can't make you. So g'on, Jahmani. I'm finna go in here and make sure Lonnie is okay. I got this." She ran her tongue across her teeth and sucked them, shook her head, and left the den.

I was so tired that I slumped on the couch and closed my eyes.

Chapter 16

"Look, Stephan, I already know how you get down, but I just want you to know my little brother didn't have nothing to do with whatever my baby daddy did. He in the trap wit' them. He got on a white hoody. He only nineteen. I don't care what you do to my baby daddy, just please spare him. I gave you all of the information you need, Stephan. Please," the dark-skinned female begged with a hood pulled over her hair. She continued to look from side to side as she sat in the back seat of a Chevy Astro van Stephan had stolen for the move we were about to take part in.

Stephan shook his head. "That's tough, shawty. Your brother was with them. You know how this shit go. An eye for an eye."

He extended his arm with a .45 in his hand. Her eyes got as big as saucers. He placed the barrel to her hoodie before she could evade him and pulled the trigger. *Boom.* Her head jerked backward. She left the back of the van a mess.

Stephan tucked the gun and drove down the alley. "Fuck that bitch, bruh. Soon as I let her go, she wasn't gon' do nothing but run and tell twelve. That bitch a yenta. She'll do anything for a bag."

He stormed down the alley and pulled the van to the side next to a dumpster, threw it in park, and rolled a mask down his face. In the passenger's seat, I did the same. I checked over my shoulder one last time and saw the dark-skinned chick with her eyes wide open. Half of her face was blown off. She still looked shocked.

"Yo, let's go in here and make this shit quick. I have another important engagement to get to." I tucked both forties and opened the van door. "How we supposed to be getting in this muthafucka, anyway?"

"This the south, homie. We gon' kick that boy in. Shawty said the door barely hanging on by the hinges, anyway. All we gotta do is rock it, and then we in there." He jumped out of the van and jogged across the alley to my side, threw his hoodie over his head, and made his way toward our targets.

It was extremely hot outside. The fact that it was nine thirty at night made no difference. I fixed the hoodie over my head as well and stayed as low as possible. We hopped the fence to the backyard and ran alongside the gangway, then we climbed the porch. I stood on the side of the door while Stephan took a few steps back and gathered himself. He raised his foot and held the sides of the door. In one hard kick, he caved in the lock. He gathered himself again and finished it off with another kick.

As soon as the door went flying, I flew inside with guns out, looking for a target. I was expecting to see a few right inside the living room, but all I saw was a deserted house. There was nothing and no one inside.

Stephan was right on my heels. He came to a halt. "Yo, what the fuck, B? Where they all at?" he asked with guns out.

Something wasn't sitting right wit' my gut. I felt butterflies. "Yo, kid, I think this a set-up. We gotta get the fuck out of here."

There was the sound of a car slamming on its brakes in front of the house. The doors opened, and seconds later the house was under attack.

Boom. Boom. Boom. Boom.

I dropped to the floor as the windows shattered. The house felt like it was stuck inside an earthquake as it rocked back and forth. I jumped up and ran to the back of the house as the shots continued.

Stephan hollered out in pain and fell to the floor. He slapped his hand over his stomach. "I'm hit. I'm hit, bruh.

Fuck."

I ducked down inside the hallway and aimed toward the front window that had been shattered.

Bocka. Bocka. Bocka. Bocka.

They sent more shots, then I heard heavy footsteps on the porch before two dudes rushed in, busting back-to-back. Stephan stood up and fired toward the pair.

Blocka. Blocka. Blocka.

He stood one up, hitting him twice in the chest. He twisted in the air and fell onto his back. The other was fortunate enough to run back outside the doorway. I could see him crouch down with a Glock in his hand. "You gon' get yours, Stephan. Every time you come down here, it's some bullshit!" he hollered. "You just kilt my cousin!" He fired into the house again.

Boom. Boom.

Bocka. Bocka. Bocka.

I shot back. "Nigga, bring yo' ass on!" I ordered Stephan. I was ready to get the fuck out of there, especially after I heard another set of brakes screeching to a halt and doors opening. Then they were running up the stairs. I didn't know who these dudes were, but it was clear they were on bidness.

Stephan held his stomach and ran toward the hallway where I was. Before he could get there, his shoulder exploded. He turned around and fired his gun as more shots came in our direction. I saw a bullet slam into his chest, and another into his stomach.

That was all I needed to see. I took off running. I didn't know that nigga like that, and I'd be damned if I stood around next to him while the both of us were killed. So, I broke into a back bedroom and jumped out the first-floor window. I thought about using the back door but figured our enemies might've been waiting patiently for us. When I jumped out and came down on the concrete in the gangway, I saw two Chevys in the front of the house with their doors opened. As if on cue, they were loaded up and screeched away from the house before storming down the street in their retreat.

Stephan burst through the back door of the house, struggling to breathe. He had blood dripping from his mouth, and his midsection was saturated with blood and bullet holes. "Jahmani, help me! Uh. Uh. Uh." He held his arms out to me, creeping across the cement. "Help me."

I stood there with my gun in hand. Just by the look of him, I could tell there was nothing that could be done to save him. He was on his way out. It was only a matter of time. "Kid, you fucked up, boss. Look at you."

He struggled to make it to me, fell to his knees, reached up for me, and coughed up a thick loogie of blood. It seeped over his bottom lip and hung like an icicle from his chin. "My suitcase. My suitcase." He coughed more blood, his eyes rolling backward. "Give my suitcase to my mama." He fell to his chest and lay with his face on the pavement. His eyes were wide open, fluttering.

I rushed over to him and dug in his pocket for his truck keys, found them, then took the stolen whip's keys from him. After I grabbed all of that, I bounced. In my opinion, there was nothing I could do for him. Life was a bitch, and she had slapped the life out of Stephan.

***

"Misty, wake yo' ass up, baby. Get up," I growled twenty minutes later.

Misty made an angry noise and slapped at my hand. "Leave me alone, Jahmani. I'm tired. Get away from me. I thought you was supposed to be over Ari's?" She pulled the sheets back over her head.

"What?" I slapped her on her fat-ass booty hard. She shot up and out of the bed in a pair of bikini-cut panties. Up top she was naked. Even in my state of panic, her titties looked so perfect and good to me wit' those big, brown nipples.

"Jahmani, what the fuck is wrong you? I just got to sleep, and I got one of the worst migraines I've ever had in my life."

"Yo, your cousin dead, shawty. I don't know what type of niggas he got into it with or what his purpose was for truly going at them, but they just smoked his ass about fifteen minutes away from here. Left him twisted in the backyard, riddled with bullets. They would've caught me slipping, too, if I hadn't busted back and got the fuck out of there."

Misty ran her fingers through her hair. Her eyes went from slits to bucked wide open. "Jahmani, don't play wit' me like that. That's not even funny. Where is Stephan?"

Lonnie turned onto her back and stretched her little arms over her head. "Uncle, I missed you." She curled up on her side and drifted back to sleep.

I picked up Stephan's suitcase and grabbed ahold of Misty's wrist, damn near dragging her from the room. We went into the room that was designated for Lonnie and I closed the door. "Shawty, now listen to me. He gone. That nigga is dead. I don't know what you finna tell Vicki, or if you're going to tell her right away, but her son is gone. We gotta get the fuck out of North Carolina, like ASAP."

Misty covered her mouth. "Oh my God. She gon' be devastated. Stephan was her everything. He was the last version of her late husband she loved. Damn."

I tossed the suitcase onto the bed and opened it. It was filled with cash. There were rubber-banded knots of hundreds and fifties everywhere I looked. I was thinking that after we hit the casino, Stephan had lied to me about giving the other people their cuts. It was either that or he hadn't had the chance to give it to them yet. "You see all of this?

Misty looked into the suitcase and covered her mouth. "Where the hell did you get all of this money? How much is it?"

"This was dude shit. It gotta be over two million dollars. He wanted me to give it to Vicki, but I ain't finna do that. Ain't she a doctor or some shit?"

Misty nodded. "Yeah, and?"

"And, we need this money to break away from this muthafucka. Besides, I busted a move wit' dude, and I was supposed to get more than what he gave me. Since he ain't here no more, I'm thinking I should keep all this shit for us."

Misty shook her head. "But he said to give it to her. Why wouldn't you listen to him?"

I sucked my teeth. "That ain't how the game go. That nigga popped, so it is what it is. He gotta take his loss. I will give her about fifty gees, though." I zipped the suitcase back. "Yo, I need you to get Lonnie dressed so we can get out of here, like, right away."

"You talking tonight?"

"Misty, I don't know yo' aunty. I don't know how she finna take this news about her son. I do know twelve finna be all over here, though. They gon' be running yo' name and mine. I ain't finna go down like that. We need to get the hell out of this state. So, let's go."

Misty sat on the edge of the bed, looking as if she was trying to gather herself. "Damn, I can't believe he's gone. I was just hollering at him, like, a hour ago. This is all so bizarre. Now we're supposed to just pick up and leave my aunt? She's going to lose her mind when she finds out he's gone. I think I need to be here to console her. If not me, then who?" She covered her face, as she had a habit of doing when she was confused and on the verge of losing her mind.

I knelt beside her. "Baby, we gotta go. We gotta get out of here. If you think about things logically, you'll see I'm right. Nothing good can come from us staying here. Now, please get up and get Lonnie together. I'm finna go and check in on Ari and get her ready."

Misty hopped up. "Wait a minute, you're about to still go over there? Are you fuckin' kidding me?"

"Hell nall, I'm not. She gotta get her ass ready to go. Until I find out whether she's pregnant with my kid, she's just as much a priority as any of us. I don't feel like arguing wit' you about this. Just please, get ready."

"Fuck that. If you're going over there to cater to her, then I'm straight. I ain't going. I'm about to go and tell my aunt that Stephan is dead and be here for her. You can go ahead and do whatever you want to do. I guess I'll catch you later." She bumped me as she attempted to walk past me.

I grabbed her by the waistband on her panties and pulled her back in front of me. "Shawty, you my muthafuckin' woman, and you carrying my seed. That means we're in all of this together. Now, I say it's time to go because I need to know you are beside me, so take yo' ass in there and get my niece ready so when I get back, we can bounce. You got a problem wit' that, oh well."

Misty smacked my hand away. "Just who in the hell do you think you are, Jahmani? Huh? You think everything is supposed to go yo' muthafuckin' way? Huh? Do you honestly think I am going to sit around and allow you to live two separate lives? You think I'm that weak. Do you?" She stepped into my face.

I snatched her ass up and picked her up off of her feet, placed her back against the wall of the room, and held her there under her arms like she really was a little-ass girl. "Misty, baby girl, listen to me. We gotta get the fuck out of North Carolina. It is only a matter of time before them people burrow down on us. I ain't trying to be booked under no circumstances. And I ain't living a double life. If Ari is pregnant, it happened before you and I happened. Now, the man in me has to make sure she's not carrying my seed. The second I confirm she isn't, I won't think twice about kicking her ass to the curb. You better believe that. I love you, and only you. Why can't you get that through your head?" She was frustrating the hell out of me.

Misty looked into my eyes and curled her upper lip. "Jahmani, you need to let me down. You're asking me why I question your love, it's because of shit like this. What type of man who loves a woman hurts her in the ways you have?"

I held her for a few more seconds and slowly placed her on her bare feet. Her pretty, French-manicured toes touched the carpet first. "What do you mean, Misty? How have I hurt you?"

She turned her back to me and ran her fingers through her curly hair. "I don't know, Jahmani. I guess I should've known better than to mess around with my cousin's man. I'm starting to feel real stupid. It's like one bad thing is happening to us after the next. I should've known what I was getting into before I did. I don't feel like you're meant for me. You might just be meant for her."

I felt sick. "Yo, so what are you saying, shawty?"

"I'm saying I no longer wanna be with you, Jahmani. I think we need to break all ties with one another. After my aunt finds out about Stephan, she's going to lose her marbles. I need to be here to hold her down. I don't think it'll be smart for me to carry on with you. I have my whole life ahead of me. You and Ari been wrecking and bodying stuff together since before me. Maybe she's your Bonnie." She lowered her head. "Damn, this sucks though."

"You damn right it do, because you're my baby. I love you, and I ain't trying to lose you for nobody. What Ari and I had was never real. I have never felt for her what I feel for you. You're my baby girl."

"No. I can't be your baby girl no more, Jahmani. It's just too much happening. We're up against way too many battles for us to be able to come out of things victorious. It's just not possible. No matter how much of a bitch Ari really is, she seems to love you. If she didn't, she wouldn't keep coming for you in the manner she has. Do I trust her? Hell no. Should you? Absolutely not. But it's like you two deserve each other."

"I deserve you. And if you leave me, what about our child?" I wanted to know. On the low I was becoming undone at the seams. I couldn't fathom losing Misty. I'd become too addicted to her. I loved the way she was always all over me. She treated me like her husband and her daddy at the same time. For me, it was a perfect blend because she was so small and so fine. At the same time, she was jazzy. I wasn't about to let her go. I didn't give a fuck what she was talking about. My love for her had grown too strong.

My phone buzzed in my pocket. Without even looking at the face, I already knew it was Ari hitting me up.

Misty sighed. "Honestly, Jahmani, I don't know what I'm going to do about it yet. I'm still mulling over some things."

"Fuck you talking about? Ain't nothing to mull over. You ain't the only one that get to make a decision about this matter. We need to come to a collective agreement. My say is just as powerful as yours."

She shook her head. "No, it's not. And when you say things like that, you only force me into a corner. I'm tired of you trying to run me and treating me like my thoughts and feelings don't matter. I've had enough of that. Whether I have this baby or not is up to me. Not you." She glared into my eyes for a few more seconds and sighed. "Look, just go to Ari. When you get back, we'll figure this situation out. I need to see how I'm going to break this other situation down to her. Still can't believe Stephan is gone."

I wanted to check her. I wanted to snap out and demand she go and get herself and Lonnie ready, but it was pointless. Misty seemed to be slipping through my fingers. The more I pushed, the further she backed away from me. I didn't want to lose her. She was my baby. "Look, Misty, I'm sorry for all of the ways I've hurt you. I swear, I didn't mean to. I really do love you, and I wanna be with you and only you. Nobody comes before you, baby. Nobody. I am begging you to get Lonnie ready so we can bounce. I need you by my side. I don't want to lose you. Can you wait to tell Vicki what's good until I get back in a hour or so?"

She was silent, shrugged her shoulders, and stepped out of the room. "I love you, too, Jahmani. More than you'll ever understand. Go ahead and do what you gotta do wit' her. I'll see you when you get back, Lord willing."

Even though she skated around my question, I saw I didn't have any other choice. I had to leave things where they were until I found out what was good with Ari. I wished Ari had never told me she was pregnant. Now that she had, I couldn't help but feel a sense of compassion and worry for her. I had to make sure she was good, even if she wasn't with me.

I grabbed twenty thousand in cash, threw it inside a pillowcase, and headed out.

Chapter 17

Ari opened the hotel door and stepped to the side. "I'm surprised you came. When it got closer to midnight, I figured you was about to stand me up. Have you eaten?"

I came inside and tossed the pillowcase on the bed. "Look, Ari, some shit done popped off, and we gotta get out of North Carolina. Now, I would like for you to come along, but I ain't gon' force you, seeing as it ain't gon' do nothing but keep up a bunch of garbage. However, it's twenty thousand dollars in that pillowcase right there. It's all yours. You can do whatever with it that you please, under one condition."

She closed the door and locked it, walked over to the night table, and picked up a glass of orange juice, downing half of it. "What's the condition, Jahmani? Huh?"

I came out of my pocket with two EPT pregnancy tests. "I want you to piss on these sticks so I can confirm you're pregnant. That's all I ask. If you are, then we have to go a whole different route with everything."

Ari looked me over from the corner of her eye. She scoffed and laughed. "You know what, Jahmani? You're a real piece of work. What the fuck do I have to gain by lying to you about being pregnant? Nigga, you are on the run. You can be taken down at any minute. You've taken more from me than you could ever give, so trust me when I tell you, me being pregnant by you is the worst case scenario. Who's putting you up to this? Is it Misty? Huh? That bitch calling shots over you now?" she laughed. "Well, I wouldn't worry about that too much longer. That bitch should be taken out of the equation, I don't know, right about now."

"Ain't nobody tell me to do nothing. I wanna know this for my own good. You told me you were pregnant, and you ain't confirmed it yet, so what's good? You gon' piss on these sticks or not?"

She smiled and held her chin. "Nigga, I don't gotta prove myself to you. That's been my problem all along. I've been trying to seek your approval by playing these crazy mind games wit' you, but I'm tired of that now, Jahmani. I'm sick of you and that bitch, Misty. You allowing her to put her hands on me was the last straw. I told you that you were going to reap what you've sown. So," she took a step back.

Beans ran out of the bathroom with two Glocks in his hands. He aimed them at me. There was a big smile spread across his ugly face. Two Korean dudes with black ski masks slid from under the bed. They were armed with Tech Nines. They took their weapons and aimed them at me as well.

Beans was the first to speak. "Well, well, well. What do we have here, Ari baby?" He pulled her to him and kissed her cheek. She frowned and tried to break free of his hold. I could tell she was uncomfortable, but nevertheless, the bitch had set me up.

I backed up and wanted to reach for my Glock bad. I was sure if I made any move, his hittas would have lit my ass up. "Beans, what the fuck this all about, homie?"

He grabbed Ari around the neck and licked her face. "Aw, you been in the game long enough to know what's good. You been set up, nigga. What, you thought just because you left New York that a muthafucka wasn't gon' find you or something?" He tossed Ari to the floor aggressively and aimed his gun at me. "You can't trust them hos, Jahmani. If it's one facet of the game you should adhere too, it's always good to honor that golden rule. Now, look at you. You fucked up. Where is Samantha?" He jerked his gun forward, and I swore I thought he let off a shot.

I tensed and clenched my jaw. "I ain't heard from her in a few months. I don't know where she at," I answered honestly.

Samantha was Lonnie's mother. She was also my brother Pacho's baby mother.

"Tsk, tsk, tsk. That's the wrong answer, right there. You see, Samantha ran off with a whole lot of my product and money. Those are losses I ain't willing to take. Somebody gon' have to compensate me for my losses. We're looking at close to two million dollars' worth of losses here, Jahmani. How are we going to reconcile that?"

"Nigga, I don't know how the fuck you gon' reconcile it. That shit ain't got nothing to do wit' me. I ain't took shit from you." I was looking for an opening to up my Glock so I could get to squeezing, but once again, they had their guns pinned on me, ready to blow my head off.

Beans stepped forward. "Who the fuck you think you talking to, li'l nigga?" Beans was dark-skinned, heavyset, and stood at about six feet, four inches tall. His hair was in dreads, and I could tell his hairline was receding horribly. It was time to cut that shit off.

I stood my ground. "Like I said, bruh, I ain't got nothing to do wit' what she did to you. She stay in her lane, and I stay in mine. That's the way the game go. That's the way it's always gone."

He grabbed me by the jacket and balled his fist into my coat, placed his gun to my forehead, and cocked the hammer. "Nigga, I said I done nearly took a two million dollar loss. A loss I ain't willing to take. Since I'm down two million, somebody owe me four million, and I betta get paid or I'm about to leave bodies all over North Carolina, starting wit' Misty, that bitch daughter, and that old ho we snatched up from the hospital. What you think about that?" He laughed out loud.

I swallowed my spit. I knew this fool wasn't saying in so many words that he had my people already. I'd just left Misty, so I knew that couldn't be the case. *Or is it?* I wondered.

"Ari, tell this nigga what I'ma do to your cousin if he don't come up with my cash in an orderly fashion." He grabbed a handful of her hair. "Tell him!"

"He gon' kill her. I'm sorry, Jahmani. Please, don't be mad at me, baby. You know I love you with all of my heart. You're my–" She busted up laughing. "Yo, my word, I can't even keep up this charade. He standing there looking stupid as hell. Pussy-nigga, we heard about that casino you hit wit' Stephan. He told me he had about two million put up somewhere. You about to take us to that money, along with the money from every other lick you hit since you've been in North Carolina, and when it's all said and done, you might leave this bitch with your life. You and Lonnie. Misty dead, though. That ho is mine."

Beans smiled. "That's why I love you, girl. You so cold-hearted, just like me." He grabbed her by the hair and tongued her down for a full two-plus minutes. The whole time he had his gun locked on me.

I had to find a way to come from under this situation. I couldn't go out like a sucka. I couldn't let my people be killed. I had to outthink the room. It was our only chance at survival. "Say, money, long as you let me and Lonnie walk away scot-free, I'll take you to that nigga stash, and you can have all of it and the li'l five hunnit gees I came up on since I been here. That shit ain't worth dying over. I just wanna raise my niece."

"What about Misty? You saying you won't give a damn if we waste her?" Ari wanted to know. She looked confused and a bit skeptical.

"Shawty too clingy, and she know way too much. We had to bust some major moves to get that money. The way I see it, you'll be doing me a favor. When we rolling out?"

Ari broke from under him. "Seriously, you gon' give her up just like that? You mean this was all just a game to you?

You never even cared about her?"

I shook my head and lied, "The only person I've ever been in love with is you. You fucked my head up, shawty. I'll never be able to recover from this."

She looked sick. Beans bumped her out of the way. "Fuck all that lovey-dovey shit. Where this money at? How soon can we get it?"

"I'll go and get that shit right now. Like I said, as long as you can promise me that me and my niece'll walk away from this whole thang unscathed, no harm, no foul."

He nodded at one of his goons. They disappeared inside the bathroom and came back out dragging a beaten Pacho. Pacho's mouth was taped. His face was swollen, and his clothes were bloodied. I didn't understand what was going on. My brother was supposed to be locked up, serving a bid.

The goon drooped him on the floor in front of Beans. I stepped back, stunned. "Pacho? Aw, shit. What y'all do to my brother, man?"

Beans kicked Pacho in the ribs and mugged me. "You been so focused in on what you got going on, Jahmani, that you didn't even know your brother been out for three weeks looking for you, and we been looking for him. Found him four days ago in Red Hook and snatched him up. That was around the same time Ari put us up on game about this li'l setup out here. It's crazy how the cards been falling into place ever since then. Now we roll up on this paper. I likes what I'm hearing." He snatched the tape off of Pacho's mouth. "Say hi to your brother, nigga. Quit being so fuckin' rude."

Pacho tried to open his eyes, but they were jammed shut. His head looked about the size of a pumpkin. "Jahmani. What's up, li'l bruh?"

I knelt beside him and ran my hand over his head. It was caked with blood almost immediately. "Pacho. Damn, man.

Why you ain't tell me you was getting out?"

He took a deep breath and exhaled it slowly. "Overcrowding, bruh. Caught me by surprise, too. How my daughter doing?" He tried to open his eyes again. They opened far enough for me to see the whites, and then he closed them again.

I felt sick on the stomach. My brother was all I had left after my mother's murder. I had visions of us doing it big together somewhere out in Vegas one day. But now that seemed more like a dream than anything else. "She good, bruh. Healthy, strong, just like her old man. She ask about you every day. She gon' run up to you and give you a big kiss as soon as she see you. Watch what I tell you."

He forced his mangled face into a smile. "That sound like music to my ears, kid. I miss my baby. She's all I think about."

Beans smacked his lips. "A'ight. That's enough of this sappy reunion. Y'all, pick him up."

Both goons rushed over and slung Pacho against the wall.

"You love your brother? Huh, Jahmani?" Beans asked, placing the barrel of his gun to Pacho's forehead.

I was in a frenzy. I couldn't lose my brother. He was my heart. "Yeah, man! Got damn, get off of this bullshit. I told you I'll take you to the money."

Beans laughed louder. "That's what I wanna hear, Jahmani, 'cause me and you finna roll out, and if we ain't back in thirty minutes, my shooters got permission to waste this clown and that bitch in the bathtub. How you like the sound of that?"

Ari stepped next to him and kissed his lips. "This how real goons get down, Jahmani. You'sa sucka. I can't believe you thought I actually fell for yo' goofy ass. That's so insulting." She rolled her eyes.

I wanted to call her every name in the book. Instead, I kept my composure. "Look, Beans, it ain't gon' come down to nothing like that. I love my brother, and I'm not gon' let you body that innocent woman in the bathroom over nothing. But now I just gotta know, if I get you all this bread, will you let my brother go free as well? I swear we can let bygones be bygones."

He smacked Pacho with the gun and knocked him to the floor. "I guess you gon' have to see when it's time, huh?" He looked down to my brother. "If we ain't back here in thirty minutes, y'all put so many bullets in this muthafucka that they can't recognize his body, then come and find me. That's an order. Ari, you coming wit' me, baby. You know you ghetto, bitch."

Ari grabbed her coat. "All day, every day. I gotchu, boo."

Ghost

Chapter 18

Beans pulled in the back of Vicki's house twenty minutes later. He threw the Oldsmobile in park and looked into the back seat at me. "Say, kid, how long it's gon' take you to go in there and get my money?"

"All I gotta do is find his stash, bruh. I got an idea of where it is. Soon as I locate it, it's all yours," I promised him.

"Baby, don't worry. I'm finna be on his hip like stretch marks. The clock is ticking. We gon' go in here and bring yo' money out to you. If anything look fishy, I'm wasting him." She pulled out a .380 and cocked it. "I hope you don't make me waste one of my bullets on you, Jahmani. I wanna use every one of these slugs on Misty." She fixed her gloves on her hands and pushed open the car door. "Let's go."

Beans smiled. "That's that Bronx shit right there, kid. Shawty that deal. Y'all hurry the fuck up."

Ari walked behind me after we got out of the whip. She poked the gun to my back and led me into the back yard, handling me all aggressive and shit. "Come on, Jahmani."

It was pitch black in the back yard. The only light came from the moon above. It felt like the temperature had dropped considerably.

She tightened her grip on my wrist. "Did you really mean that shit you said about loving me?"

I nodded. "I been in love wit' you since day one, Ari, and I ain't just saying that shit because you got a gun to my back. It's always been you. You just fucked me when you shook me for that fool P.T. Not to mention this shit. But even still, I see that queen in you. That why I could never call you a bitch like Beans do. You're supposed to be my Eve."

She held her silence and continued to lead. "I'm nobody's Eve, Jahmani. I am a bitch. Don't nobody give a real care about me, and you shouldn't, either. It'll save you a lot of pain. Now, do what I tell you and you won't get hurt." She poked the gun into my back again and forced me to put a li'l pep in my step. "And, for the record, that 'bitch' word don't get to me. When you're raised in the gutters like I was and have been called some of the most deplorable things by your own parents, the 'bitch' word is by far one of the nicest names I've been called."

"Yeah, well, that may be so, but you're still a queen to me, and I love you. Always will, too."

When I came to the patio door of the house, I slid it to the side and stepped inside. Ari tightened her hold and placed her lips on my ear. "Jahmani, you bet not try nothing stupid. Now, I don't really want to hurt you, but if I have to, I swear I'll smoke you in a heartbeat. I refuse to face Beans for some dumb shit you've attempted. That ain't happening. You got that, kid?"

"I got that, although I would never use you like this nigga using you, Ari. You see, I came over to make sure you were good. I've had a crazy night. Lost Stephan to the gun, and I still made my way over to you to make sure you were good. That's what love is." I was trying to say all the things to strike an emotional nerve in her. In the back of my mind, I was hoping for one opportunity to get that gun away from her so I could waste her ass. I was going to take care of Beans next for how he had Pacho, and I assumed Vicki, hemmed up.

"Jahmani, just shut up and keep moving. That's all you need to do. And who do you think put Stephan down? Huh? He ran his mouth way too much. Now, take me to the stash." She pushed me into the house and caused me to stumble. I kept my hands held at shoulder height, just waiting on my moment.

The house was quiet. I wondered where Misty and Lonnie were. It was closer to one in the morning. When I'd left, Misty seemed extremely tired until she found out Stephan had been killed. I was praying she'd taken Lonnie and fled from the house. If anything happened to any one of my girls, I was going to lose my mind.

We came to the bottom of the stairs, and I looked up them. I'd left the bag of money inside Lonnie's room closet, pushed all the way to the back of it. It had to be well over two million, or at least close to that. I didn't know if I trusted giving Beans my scratch. He seemed like a dirty nigga, like once he got his cheese, he would waste all parties involved. In fact, I was sure he would.

"Let's go, Jahmani. What the hell are you waiting on?" Ari asked through clenched teeth.

"Nothin'. Come on." I kept my hands raised and took one step after the next. They creaked under my footsteps. Every time one sounded, I worried about Misty or Lonnie popping up out of nowhere and Ari shooting them. I was so worried about that my heart was pounding in my chest worse than ever. I had to get that gun out of Ari's hands.

When we made it to the top of the stairs, she wrapped her arm around my throat from the back and really jammed her gun into my back. "Which one of these rooms hold his stash? Huh? Don't forget we're on the clock here."

She tightened her grip around my Adam's Apple. This pissed me off. I pointed at Vicki's room. "In there. It should be in the wall of the closet in there." My voice was raspy because she was choking me, or at least that's what it felt like.

"Well, let's go then," she ordered.

We slowly made our way down the hall until we came upon Vicki's door. When we got in front of it, I reached out and grabbed the knob. I twisted my neck. "Baby, you choking the shit out of me," I croaked. "Loosen this hold a li'l bit. I ain't going nowhere."

She did as I asked and started to force me into the room.

As soon as we came past the threshold of Vicki's room, Lonnie stepped out of the bathroom. "Uncle!"

Ari turned to aim the gun at her. She bit into her bottom lip as if she was getting ready to fire. "Li'l bitch, you scared the shit out of me."

Lonnie saw the gun and screamed. She ran back into the bathroom and slammed the door.

Misty opened our bedroom door, rubbing her eyes. "What the hell is going on out here?"

Ari let go of me and held the gun with two hands. "Bitch, you finna die right here and right now."

Misty threw her hands into the air. "Ari, please, you ain't gotta do this. I'm sorry."

"Nall, fuck that. You'sa turncoat." She fired the silenced .380.

Boof. Boof. Boof. Boof. Boof.

Misty flew backward into the wall of the hallway and fell to the floor. She curled into a ball. I stood frozen. Ari stood over her and pulled the trigger three more times.

I expected Misty's body to be filled with holes, for blood to seep out of her, but when nothing happened, I grew irate.

Ari looked at her gun and frowned. "What the fuck? Beans and his blanks. He didn't trust me."

I slapped her so hard she flew into the wall. The gun slid across the carpet.

Misty stood up with tears in her eyes. She ran her hands over her nightgown and saw herself to still be intact. This made the tears flow down her cheeks harder. "You silly bitch. You tried to kill me. I'm tired of this shit!" She rushed Ari at full speed.

Ari was getting up off one knee. Misty tackled her to the floor and began raining blows on her, one after the other. "I hate you. I hate you. I hate you. I hate you. I hate you. I hate you." Punch after punch. Blow after blow. Ari's head ricocheted off the carpet time and time again. Finally, she twisted her hips and humped upward, tossing Misty off of her. Misty fell on her back, kicking her legs wildly.

Ari staggered to her feet. "I'm sorry. I don't wanna do this, but Beans got my mother. He got my mother, and he's going to kill her if I don't do what he says. Please, listen to me." She held her hands in front of her with blood dripping from her nose and mouth. "Please, don't hurt me no more."

Misty rushed her again, swinging wildly. "Bitch, you lying. You tried to kill me."

She caught Ari in the chin, the face, and nose, then pushed her as hard as she could toward the stairwell. Ari tumbled down the stairs and fell on her back. She lay there for a minute and jumped up, crying.

"Jahmani, you have to believe me. Beans is nuts. That fool Linx is in town, too. I don't know where he is, but if you don't get Beans his money, it's going to be hell to pay." She wiped the blood from her mouth and ran out the back door.

"Ari, wait!" Linx? How the fuck had him and Beans hooked up? The Bronx was getting crazy. I pulled my Glock and cocked it.

Misty frowned and tapped on the bathroom door. "Lonnie. Baby, it's okay. You can come out now. We're going to leave."

"I'm scared. That woman out there is going to get me," Lonnie whined.

"She's gone, baby. I swear. It's just me and your uncle Jahmani out here." She tapped on the door again. "Come on."

Lonnie slowly opened the door and peeked out of it. When she saw Misty's face, she opened it all the way and ran into her arms.

Boom. Boom.

The gunshots came from outside of the house, then there were tires squealing away.

Lonnie hugged Misty tighter. Misty rubbed her back. "It's okay, baby. It's okay. Everything is going to be alright."

I made my way down the stairs with my gun in hand. I crept through the downstairs of the house and searched for any intruders. "Ari. Ari," I whispered. There was no response. I continued to slowly make my way through the house on high alert. When I got to the back door, I stepped into the backyard and looked around. Except for the sound of crickets, everything was quiet and seemed normal.

I traveled in the direction of Beans' car, expecting him and Ari to be standing in the alley having a conversation about what to do next. Instead I saw her lying in the middle of it. I ran at full speed until I got to her side, knelt down, and looked her over. Ari shook on the pavement. She'd been shot twice in the chest. Her right hand was placed over one of the gunshot wounds that was leaking heavily.

"It's over, Jahmani. Beans finna kill everybody." She took a deep breath and tears poured out of her eyes.

I picked up her head just a bit, held it on my lap, and stroked her hair. "Ari, what the fuck, ma? Why? Why was you fuckin' wit' that nigga, fo' real? Tell me!"

She opened her mouth and jerked. Blood oozed out of it. "He. He got my mother. I'm sorry, Jahmani. I love you. Don't trust…." Her eyes rolled into the back of her head before she passed out and away.

I held her for a few minutes, then closed her eyes, kissed her on the forehead, and got up. I looked both ways and jogged back to the house.

When I got inside, Misty was packing like crazy while

Lonnie sat on the bed eating a bag of Flaming Hot Cheetos. It was her go-to food when she needed to calm down. My brother Pacho was the same way whenever he needed to calm down or think.

"Jahmani, we gotta get the hell out of here. I don't know where my aunt is, but I'm freaking out right now. Everything just seems all wrong." She zipped the suitcase and sat on the bed, laid on her back, and pulled a pair of capris up her thick thighs.

"I agree. Ari said that nigga Linx floating around, too. Before I left the hotel, they had Pacho hemmed up, and Vicki, too. At least, I think it's her. I guess they snatched her up from the hospital or somethin'. All this shit is weird."

"Yeah, tell me about it. Come on, let's get up out of here. Go get the money," she directed.

"A'ight."

I rushed into Lonnie's room and grabbed the suitcase out of the closet, unzipped it, and peeked inside. Sure enough, it was filled with cash just like I'd left it. I zipped it back up and met Misty in the hallway, took ahold of her hand, and we stomped down the stairs with Lonnie in tow.

***

Misty got behind the wheel of Vicki's Land Rover and backed it out of the garage. "We should've never brought these problems onto my aunt, Jahmani. This isn't fair. She didn't have nothing to do with any of this bullshit." She shook her head. "I know them Bronx niggas gon' kill her. If they'll do Ari like that, what chance does she have at survival?"

"I know, baby. They got my brother, too. I can't let them kill my brother. I just can't."

"So, what are we going to do? Are we going to leave North

Carolina with things the way they are, or are we going to go back and try to make things right?"

I hung my head and tried to think logically. "They in the Hilton, right?"

"I guess. I don't know where they are. You've never taken me with you."

"Yeah, that's where Ari was put up at, so that's where they are. Now, the Hilton is a luxurious hotel, and they got cameras everywhere. We can't bum-rush them on killa shit because twelve'll snatch our ass up before we can do anything. Beans gave them the order that if we don't return in a half hour with him and his money, they were to kill Pacho and Vicki. It's been forty-five minutes." My heart dropped into my stomach. "Baby, as much as it pains me to say it, I think our people are already dead."

"So, what does that mean? What are you saying?" she asked with her voice cracking.

"I'm saying I think it's in our best interest to get up out of this city before we're fucked over. There is nothing else to fight for here." My heart was super heavy for Pacho and for Vicki.

Misty shook her head. "This all just feels so wrong, Jahmani. It doesn't feel right. I'm so confused."

When I looked into the back of the truck, I saw Lonnie was knocked out asleep already. She snored lightly with her head tilted to one side. I smiled. At least my niece was safe and sound. That was very important to me. "So, what do you wanna do? Because I say we cut our losses. Lonnie is safe. You're safe. Our unborn child is safe. And I'm safe. I mean, what more can we really ask for?"

While asking this question, my phone vibrated.

"I'm just gon' leave. You're right. If they're already gone, then we have to get the hell out of here. It's only a matter of time before the walls come crashing down on us."

"Hold that thought, baby." I answered the call and put my phone on speaker. "What's good?"

"Fuck you mean, 'what's good'? Nigga, you got my money, or am I wasting this bitch and yo' brother?" Beans snapped.

"Beans, my aunty ain't have nothing to do wit' none of this. You need to let her go. We'll bring you your fuckin' money. That ain't a problem," Misty hollered.

"Yo, kid, where is my brother? If Pacho good, let me speak to him," I said, feeling a migraine come pounding inside my head.

"Nigga, I ain't letting you hear shit. If you wanna hear from Pacho, you'll bring me my paper, or else he gon' wind up like Samantha." He was quiet for a second. "Matter fact, say, Dunn. Bring me that bitch."

Misty pulled the truck to the side of the road. She turned down the air conditioner and looked over at my phone. I could see her shaking. She looked scared and worried.

"Say something, bitch. Your niece on the phone, and she's the only one that can save you right now." There was a loud smacking sound.

"Ah! Hello? Misty?" Vicki cried.

Misty squeezed her eyelids together and shook her head from side to side. "Yes, aunty?"

"Help me, baby. Please, don't let this man kill me like he did this boy. He—"

She was cut short. There was a series of slaps.

Misty lay her forehead on the steering wheel. She began to sob. "I'm so sorry, aunty. I'm so, so sorry."

There was crackling on the phone, then Beans returned. "Don't be sorry, bitch. Just get me my money. I'm texting you the address of where to meet me. Be there in a half hour or find your aunt and Pacho's body twisted. It's that simple." The call ended.

Chapter 19

"What are we going to do, Jahmani? What are we going to do?" Misty asked, pacing back and forth on the sidewalk. Her yellow face was red with tears. "I can't let him kill my aunty like that. That nigga acting like he ain't got no good sense at all."

"Yo, I think he offed Pacho already. Vicki sounded like she slipped up and told us that before he snatched her off the phone and put hands on her. If that nigga killed my brother, baby, man, I don't know what I'm finna do."

"Samantha gone, too. He used whatever happened to her to threaten you with. Beans ain't right. I feel like we're stuck right now. If we try and help your brother and my aunt, we walk into a death trap. He'll have us right where he wants us. On the other hand, if we leave them to fend for themselves, he will kill them, and then we run the risk of their deaths being on our conscience for the rest of our lives."

"I think my brother already dead, and if that's the case, Beans gotta pay for what he did. I'll do the drop-off on my own. You ain't gotta come with me. I'ma have you drop me off a block before we get to the warehouse. You need to take the money and Lonnie and get the hell out of here. I got this. I'll answer for my own sins. Let's roll."

Misty grabbed my arm. "Daddy, are you out of your mind? We're pregnant. You have a whole-ass niece in the back seat that needs you. I can't take care of her and our child all by myself. I mean, I probably could, but I shouldn't have to." She looked over to the truck and into the back window. "That is a beautiful little girl. We need you, so you're not going anywhere. We gotta let this go, Jahmani. This is what we wanted anyway, remember?"

"Remember what?" I was curious. I kept seeing Pacho's

face in my mind. I was wishing I knew if my brother was alive or not. I had that vengeful shit in my heart. I felt like I needed to go at Beans with everything I had, not to mention Linx, because that fool was still out there floating around.

"When all of this started, Jahmani, before we went to meet Ari, our sole purpose was to rescue Lonnie and get her the hell out of there. Well, look, Jahmani. She's safe, daddy. She's protected, and so are we. We have two million dollars in cash to start a whole new life. I mean, it sucks that my aunt has to be sacrificed, but there is no telling what trap we're going to walk into. Our best bet is to get the hell out of North Carolina tonight." She stepped up to me and slid her arms through my waist. "I love you, daddy. Please hear me out."

I hugged her to me. "I lost my moms, baby girl. I lost my mother, Samantha, and now I'm about to lose my brother. That's a lot of losing. I need you to know this shit is never going to be easy for me. I'm used to going at a nigga's chin for offending my people. But," I looked into her pretty eyes that had tears running out of them, "some things are much more important. I'm ready to leave this life alone, baby. I can't win every battle. Let's get the fuck out of here."

I rushed to the truck and jumped behind the steering wheel. "Where we headed?"

"I say we head west. I got a cousin in Los Angeles that'll help us get out of the states for good. Maybe we can build a life south of the border. How does that sound to you?" she asked, placing her seatbelt across her chest.

I threw the truck in drive and my seatbelt clicked into place. "I say we do it. As long as I got you and my princess back there, don't nothing else matter."

"Don't forget about the one in my oven. You already know that—"

Bam.

The truck jerked forward so hard my head slammed into the steering wheel, causing the horn to go off. *Beep.* My neck popped. Lonnie started to scream at the top of her lungs. I looked into the rearview mirror in time to see Linx and Beans hop out of a black Yukon Denali. The front end of the truck was bent inward. Both men were armed.

Misty sat in the passenger's seat to the right of me with her eyes closed. Her face rested on the airbag that deployed from the dashboard.

I turned the truck off and then on again. That way I would be able to pull off, even with the airbags deployed the way they were. I threw the truck into drive and pulled off.

Boom. Boom. Boom. Boom. Boom. Boom. Boom.

The back window to the truck exploded. Lonnie screamed at the top of her lungs as the glass went all over her face and into her hair. "Uncle! Uncle! Uncle! Help me!"

I stepped on the gas. "I got you, baby. Just hold on. Hold on for me, please!" My neck felt like it had been hit with a billy club. The pain was excruciating. I glanced to my right again. Misty was knocked out cold. A trickle of blood slid down her face.

"Baby, wake up! Wake up!" I hollered.

The Denali sped up close to my back bumper. Linx hung out of the window with an Uzi in his hand. He aimed and fired.

Pop. Pop. Pop. Pop. Pop.

The window to the driver's side door was the next to go. More shots rang out. This caused me to swerve the truck. Lonnie fell on the floor. Misty remained knocked out.

The Denali was beside us again with Linx firing his Uzi rapidly. He pulled a clip from the bottom of it and tossed it inside their truck, then he smacked a new one inside it and began busting again.

I slammed on the brakes, and their truck continued flying

forward. Smoke came from the tires. I could hear Lonnie in the background, crying her little heart out. I made a U-turn and stepped on the gas, headed back down the busy street in the opposite direction. Looking in my rearview mirror, I could see Beans making a U-turn as well.

"Misty! Misty! Wake up!" I slapped her shoulder, and this jarred her awake. She threw her head back.

"Ow, my neck!" She held it. "What happened to me?"

Beans appeared to be getting closer. Instead of Linx sitting on the windowsill of the Denali, now he was back inside it with his head and the Uzi hanging out of the window. He began firing again.

"What the hell is going on, daddy?" Misty shouted.

Lonnie screamed, "They trying to kill us! They been trying to kill us ever since you've been 'sleep!"

Misty looked into the back of the truck and her eyes got big. "Holy fuck! It's always something. It's always something, daddy!"

Pop. Pop. Pop. Pop. Pop.

Linx fired. I could tell he was out for blood. I didn't know how or when he'd linked up with Beans, but they were a deadly combination. I had to find a way to shake them. Our lives depended on it.

We flew past a red light just as a slew of cars stormed down the street, barely missing us. I looked into my rearview mirror and saw Beans was caught at the light. I took the next right and stormed down an alley, slamming on the brakes again. "Y'all, get out!"

"What!" Misty screamed.

"Baby, just be quiet and listen to me. I need y'all to get out so I can finish these niggas. As long as they know y'all are in the truck, we're their prey. I need to be predator real quick so I can save my family, so get out of the trucks and y'all run up in that garage right there. Just wait for me. Come on, now."

I clicked her seatbelt loose. The truck started to make the *ding, ding, ding* sound to indicate there was a person in the car without their seatbelt on. Misty rushed back and got Lonnie.

"Take the suitcase, too. Just hold the money," I ordered. Misty rushed to the front of the truck and kissed my lips. "I love you, daddy. Please come back safely to me."

"I got this, boo. After this, no more crime. Just our family. I promise." I kissed her again, and then Lonnie. "Now, y'all go."

***

The truck jetted out of the alley and, as if on cue, slammed directly into the side door of Beans' Denali. I hit his ass so hard it bent the door inward. I kept my foot on the gas, forcing them sideways until their truck flipped on its side.

I hopped out of mine with the Glock in hand, aiming and ready to put an end to their calendars. Beans was the first to emerge from the busted back window of the Denali with blood leaking out of his skull. "Uh. Uh. Uh. You son of a bitch." He came to his feet and staggered. "All I wanted was my muthafuckin' money." He reached on his waist.

I aimed with one eye closed and sent two shots in his direction. Both landed in his face and knocked chunks from it. He twisted around and fell on his side, lifeless. A spark came from the bottom of their truck.

"Get yo' punk-ass out, Linx! Come on, nigga. Take this shit like a man!" I hollered, hearing the sirens somewhere off in the distance.

He slowly made his way out of the passenger's window. His face was covered in blood. A fire spread across the truck. He stumbled as he stood and put up his guards. "Come on,

Jahmani. I ain't scared of you. You next on my list. I kilt Samantha. Sliced that bitch from ear to ear 'cause she wouldn't tell me where you was. Then yo' brother. I always hated Pacho. That nigga thought he was so hard. He screamed like a bitch when I sliced and diced his punk-ass. Woulda put two in Ari face if Beans hadn't got there first, but I choked Vicki's ass out. So, it's yo' turn. What you wanna do, nigga? I ain't scared. What you wanna do?" He took off running toward me.

I aimed and finger-fucked my trigger. The first and second bullet split his forehead. The third and fourth knocked holes in his chest. The fifth and sixth swept him off his feet and left him shaking on the pavement.

I stood over him and cheesed. "Take the rest of this magazine, Cover Girl."

Boom. Boom. Boom. Boom.

His body leapt from the pavement over and over, and then I took off running.

***

Two Years Later

Havana, Cuba

Misty walked across the white sand with her long hair flowing past her shoulders. She carried our son, Damani, in her arms. She walked over to me and placed him in my arms as the waves from the ocean crashed onto the beach.

"Here, baby. This boy driving me crazy. He want me to carry him all day long. Got my arms hurting. Now he wanna be 'sleep." She rolled her eyes.

I laughed and kissed my son on the forehead. "He just love his mama, what can I say? If he kicking yo' tail, what you gon' do when our next one come?" I rubbed her stomach as she lay down next to me, pregnant and looking fine as ever. The sunlight glistened off of her wedding ring. Misty had been my wife for eighteen months, and I'd never felt happier.

"I don't know, but I got four more months to figure it out."

"It's all good, aunty. You know I got your back. We're a family, and we're all in this together," Lonnie said, smiling.

I agreed. Long as we had each other, nothing else mattered.

The End.

Submission Guideline

Submit the first three chapters of your completed manuscript to ldpsubmissions@gmail.com, subject line: Your book's title. The manuscript must be in a .doc file and sent as an attachment. Document should be in Times New Roman, double spaced and in size 12 font. Also, provide your synopsis and full contact information. If sending multiple submissions, they must each be in a separate email.

Have a story but no way to send it electronically? You can still submit to LDP/Ca$h Presents. Send in the first three chapters, written or typed, of your completed manuscript to:

LDP: Submissions Dept
Po Box 870494
Mesquite, Tx 75187

DO NOT send original manuscript. Must be a duplicate.

Provide your synopsis and a cover letter containing your full contact information.

Thanks for considering LDP and Ca$h Presents.

Coming Soon from Lock Down Publications/Ca$h Presents

BOW DOWN TO MY GANGSTA

By **Ca$h**

TORN BETWEEN TWO

By **Coffee**

BLOOD STAINS OF A SHOTTA **III**

By **Jamaica**

STEADY MOBBIN **III**

By **Marcellus Allen**

BLOOD OF A BOSS **V**

By **Askari**

LOYAL TO THE GAME **IV**

LIFE OF SIN II

By **T.J. & Jelissa**

A DOPEBOY'S PRAYER **II**

By **Eddie "Wolf" Lee**

IF LOVING YOU IS WRONG... **III**

LOVE ME EVEN WHEN IT HURTS **III**

By **Jelissa**

TRUE SAVAGE **VII**

By **Chris Green**

BLAST FOR ME **III**

DUFFLE BAG CARTEL III

By **Ghost**

ADDICTIED TO THE DRAMA **III**

By **Jamila Mathis**

Ghost

A Bronx Tale 3

STEADY MOBBIN' **III**
Marcellus Allen
SINS OF A HUSTLA II
ASAD
TRIGGADALE II
Elijah R. Freeman
MARRIED TO A BOSS II
By Destiny Skai & Chris Green
KINGS OF THE GAME II
Playa Ray

Available Now
RESTRAINING ORDER **I & II**
By **CA$H & Coffee**
LOVE KNOWS NO BOUNDARIES **I II & III**
By **Coffee**
RAISED AS A GOON I, II, III & IV
BRED BY THE SLUMS I, II, III
BLAST FOR ME I & II
ROTTEN TO THE CORE I III
A BRONX TALE I, II, III
DUFFEL BAG CARTEL I II
By **Ghost**
LAY IT DOWN **I & II**
LAST OF A DYING BREED
BLOOD STAINS OF A SHOTTA I & II

Ghost

By **Jamaica**
LOYAL TO THE GAME
LOYAL TO THE GAME II
LOYAL TO THE GAME III
LIFE OF SIN
By **TJ & Jelissa**
BLOODY COMMAS I & II
SKI MASK CARTEL I II & III
KING OF NEW YORK I II,III IV
RISE TO POWER I II
By **T.J. Edwards**
IF LOVING HIM IS WRONG…I & II
LOVE ME EVEN WHEN IT HURTS I II
By **Jelissa**
WHEN THE STREETS CLAP BACK I & II III
By **Jibril Williams**
A DISTINGUISHED THUG STOLE MY HEART I II & III
LOVE SHOULDN'T HURT I II III
RENEGADE BOYS I & II
By **Meesha**
A GANGSTER'S CODE I &, II III
By **J-Blunt**
PUSH IT TO THE LIMIT
By **Bre' Hayes**
BLOOD OF A BOSS **I, II, III & IV**
By **Askari**
THE STREETS BLEED MURDER **I, II & III**

THE HEART OF A GANGSTA I II& III

By **Jerry Jackson**

CUM FOR ME

CUM FOR ME 2

CUM FOR ME 3

CUM FOR ME 4

An **LDP Erotica Collaboration**

BRIDE OF A HUSTLA **I II & II**

THE FETTI GIRLS **I, II& III**

CORRUPTED BY A GANGSTA I, II & III

By **Destiny Skai**

WHEN A GOOD GIRL GOES BAD

By **Adrienne**

THE COST OF LOYALTY

By Kweli

A GANGSTER'S REVENGE **I II III & IV**

THE BOSS MAN'S DAUGHTERS

THE BOSS MAN'S DAUGHTERS II

THE BOSSMAN'S DAUGHTERS III

THE BOSSMAN'S DAUGHTERS IV

THE BOSS MAN'S DAUGHTERS **V**

A SAVAGE LOVE **I & II**

BAE BELONGS TO ME I II

A HUSTLER'S DECEIT I, II, III

WHAT BAD BITCHES DO I, II

By **Aryanna**

A KINGPIN'S AMBITON

A KINGPIN'S AMBITION **II**

I MURDER FOR THE DOUGH

By **Ambitious**

TRUE SAVAGE

TRUE SAVAGE II

TRUE SAVAGE **III**

TRUE SAVAGE **IV**

TRUE SAVAGE **V**

TRUE SAVAGE **VI**

By **Chris Green**

A DOPEBOY'S PRAYER

By **Eddie "Wolf" Lee**

THE KING CARTEL **I, II & III**

By **Frank Gresham**

THESE NIGGAS AIN'T LOYAL **I, II & III**

By **Nikki Tee**

GANGSTA SHYT **I II &III**

By **CATO**

THE ULTIMATE BETRAYAL

By **Phoenix**

BOSS'N UP **I , II & III**

By **Royal Nicole**

I LOVE YOU TO DEATH

By Destiny J

I RIDE FOR MY HITTA

I STILL RIDE FOR MY HITTA

By **Misty Holt**

LOVE & CHASIN' PAPER

By **Qay Crockett**

TO DIE IN VAIN

SINS OF A HUSTLA

By **ASAD**

BROOKLYN HUSTLAZ

By **Boogsy Morina**

BROOKLYN ON LOCK I & II

By **Sonovia**

GANGSTA CITY

By **Teddy Duke**

A DRUG KING AND HIS DIAMOND I & II III

A DOPEMAN'S RICHES

HER MAN, MINE'S TOO I, II

CASH MONEY HO'S

By **Nicole Goosby**

TRAPHOUSE KING **I II & III**

KINGPIN KILLAZ I II III

STREET KINGS

By **Hood Rich**

LIPSTICK KILLAH **I, II**

CRIME OF PASSION I & II

By **Mimi**

STEADY MOBBN' **I, II**

By **Marcellus Allen**

WHO SHOT YA **I, II**

Renta

GORILLAZ IN THE BAY **I II**

DE'KARI

TRIGGADALE

Elijah R. Freeman

GOD BLESS THE TRAPPERS I, II, III

THESE SCANDALOUS STREETS I, II, III

FEAR MY GANGSTA I, II, III

THESE STREETS DON'T LOVE NOBODY I, II

BURY ME A G I, II, III, IV, V

A GANGSTA'S EMPIRE I, II, III

Tranay Adams

THE STREETS ARE CALLING

Duquie Wilson

MARRIED TO A BOSS...

By Destiny Skai & Chris Green

KINGS OF THE GAME II

Playa Ray

BOOKS BY LDP'S CEO, CA$H

TRUST IN NO MAN
TRUST IN NO MAN 2
TRUST IN NO MAN 3
BONDED BY BLOOD
SHORTY GOT A THUG
THUGS CRY
THUGS CRY 2
THUGS CRY 3
TRUST NO BITCH
TRUST NO BITCH 2
TRUST NO BITCH 3
TIL MY CASKET DROPS
RESTRAINING ORDER
RESTRAINING ORDER 2
IN LOVE WITH A CONVICT

Coming Soon
BONDED BY BLOOD 2
BOW DOWN TO MY GANGSTA

Ghost